THE FALL

Karma Police Book Five

SEAN PLATT

DAVID W. WRIGHT

STERLING & STONE

THE FALL

Prologue

ELLA

~

MY FATHER'S comment echoes in my head.

You're not Ella. I buried Ella years ago.

"No, I *am* her," I cry out. "I know it. I have her memories. I remember you. I'm a Jumper."

He grabs my hand, pulling me through his bedroom, then a door in the back, and into a dark, smaller room with nothing but a round table and five chairs.

Papers, pens, and maps are scattered all over the table, along with half empty bottles of soda and alcohol. A planning room of some sort.

He puts his gun on the table with a thud. "What else do you remember?"

"I don't know. Bits of this and that, but not much that makes sense."

He must see something in my eyes. He seems to relax.

"We probably don't have long. I'm sure that they're using you to find me."

"Who?"

"Fairchild."

I swallow. "I told him I'd talk to you. He said he wouldn't, that he couldn't follow you."

"Yeah, he lied. Once a Jumper has a location, they can home in on us."

"I'm so sorry," I say. "I'll talk to him."

"He doesn't want to *talk*."

"What *does* he want?"

"To bury his secrets. To hide the things he's done. To kill The First Front. But most of all, he wants someone I'm hiding. Someone he needs so he can do something terrible. So, you really think you're Ella?"

I nod. "Aren't I?"

"No."

"Then who am I?"

"You're asking the wrong question. It's not who, it's what."

"What?"

"I may as well share it all with you. I have a feeling I might not make it out of this alive, and there ought to be *some record*."

"Record of what?"

He quickly steps toward me.

I flinch.

"It's okay," he says, placing his palms on either side of my head like he's about to give my scalp a massage.

His eyes, piercing blue, meet mine. They're kind, though weary. "Are you ready?"

"For what?"

"To remember."

"Yes."

Then the memories surge, from his mind to mine.

And I'm no longer in my body, or even in the present.

I'm in his, as a child.

Chapter One

Ben Shepherd Age 12

THERE ARE times when I can feel Fate humming, a vague stirring as its various mechanisms kick into gear, sounding almost like a computer powering up from its slumber. It *thrums* in my body. There's an electricity in the air, and the hairs on my arm and neck stand on end.

I can tell that something terrible is about to happen.

I can feel it now as I stand in the lunch line with Timmy Spooner, one of my only friends in the world.

Timmy's in front of me pretending to debate between the pizza and the prepared salads as if the salad has any hope. I love Timmy like a brother, but he's fat and doesn't want to change, so why go through the pretense? Does he think I'll judge him if he indulges in bad food? I'm not like the other jerks in this school.

I look around, trying to find the source of the

humming. Looking for the bad thing that's about to happen, and, more importantly, who it will happen to.

But I never see what's going to happen or who it will happen to ahead of time. It's a general feeling, and, if I'm lucky, I'll happen to look in the right place at the right time.

Sometimes I'll see someone about to take a nasty fall. A few times I've seen servers drop entire trays of food shortly after the humming. The worst thing I've seen so far was the time I heard the hum and happened to look at the intersection near the playground by my house to see an old lady about to cross the street with her dog. I had a feeling that something bad was about to happen, but I couldn't see any threats.

And then, on a clear day with barely any wind, a giant tree fell on her, instantly killing the old lady *and* her dog.

I never had a chance to intervene.

And that's the problem with this secret "gift" as my father calls it. It doesn't help anyone. I never seem to see anything that relates to *my* future, or anyone around me. I see vague snippets of stuff I can't do anything about. Mostly, I get an anxious feeling that something will happen in my general vicinity.

Useless.

I'm not like my father, who was born with abilities that help him do his job at Advanced Dynamics. He hasn't even told me what his gift is, or much about his job beyond his title as *researcher*, but I know his gift helps him stop bad people from doing terrible things.

Dad says we're different from most other people, and we can't ever tell anyone about our abilities. Nor am I ever supposed to use my gift around others, not that I would even know how. It more or less uses me, as far as I can tell.

My gift is an annoyance, and one that comes with crippling headaches. I'd be the worst superhero ever — *Migraine Boy!*

Fortunately, I haven't had a bad one in two years.

I look at the line of kids both in front and behind us but see nothing out of place.

I look at the cafeteria workers milling about, carrying hot trays to the line, others in the back preparing meals, and the cashier, sitting on her chair waiting for a boy to dig money out of his jeans.

I can't see any obvious problems about to unfold. I wonder if something might happen to me?

But I never get a warning that I'm about to be tripped or jumped by some assholes looking to prove something.

What if the thing that's going to happen to me is so bad that this time I *am* getting a warning?

I think about my earlier run-in with Rick Russo — a jock whose had it in for Timmy for years. Rick was trying to start a fight at the bus stop this morning, gently shoving Timmy, trying to get him to swing, calling him a pussy when he wouldn't fight back.

Rick's friends laughed, calling Timmy every terrible name.

Tired of standing by, I stepped up to Rick and told him to back off. That earned *oohs* and *ahs* from the other kids swarming like sharks smelling blood in the water.

I could feel the electricity, and a part of me welcomed it. I *wanted* a chance to knock Rick on his ass.

But then the bus came and paused the fight.

Rick pointed at me. "Don't think this is over, faggot."

As Timmy and I boarded the bus, sitting in the front, near the driver like we always did, Timmy whispered, "What were you thinking? He's going to kill you."

I wasn't worried much about it. I've been in fights before, and usually find my way out of them, either verbally or with a few good moves my father has taught me over the years. But I was relatively new at this school, and they assumed I was a wimp because of my stature and desire to lay low.

And, for the first time, I feel a gnawing in my gut that maybe I pushed Rick too far. That I did something that's going to screw everything up for either Timmy or me.

Timmy finally tells the woman behind the counter, "I'll have pizza."

I laugh, thankful for a distraction from my morbid thoughts.

Timmy shoots me a look. "*What?*"

"Nothing," I say, raising my hands.

"I'm not a fat ass," he thinks.

I can also pick up on people's thoughts sometimes, even though I never try. Well, that's sort of a lie. I have tried to a few times, particularly when I was wondering if a girl liked me or if I was in trouble with a teacher. But, as with the visions, I have no control.

Timmy moves down the line to his next choice. My money is on the big ass oatmeal raisin cookie. The fruit cup might as well be a turd.

I feel like a hypocrite putting the pizza on my tray. Not that I have to worry about my weight. I'm rail thin, which makes my friendship with Timmy a source of jokes for the kids that pick on us. We've heard many calls of "fatty and skinny" while walking the halls.

And this time I thought things would be different.

But no matter how many times we move for my dad's job, kids are always cruel.

At least this time, I have a comrade in Timmy, a fellow geek to commiserate with, and sometimes laugh at the others with. Nothing quite like mocking your tormenters to forge a bond.

We make our way down the line and pay for our meals. Still, nothing's happened.

The hum is louder. I'm looking around the entire cafeteria, wondering who will be the recipient of whatever Fate has in store.

I follow Timmy to the table nearest the teachers — that's where we're least likely to get messed with by the assholes who usually favor the rear of the cafeteria. That way, they are closest to the back doors, where they sneak out to do whatever it is that asshole kids do when teachers aren't around to watch.

Timmy and I sit at the table next to one another like we usually do, our backs to the teachers' tables so we have a good view of the entire cafeteria.

Sometimes you'll see jocks looking to mess with you. Make eye contact, and you're screwed. But if you saw them coming, you could pretend to be reading or engaged in a conversation — anything that might allow you to blend in.

This time I'm not looking for trouble to avoid so much as a disaster in the making. I wonder who it will happen to, and how bad it will be. From a bloody nose to the death of an old woman and her dog, the volume of the hum isn't dependent on severity.

As Timmy goes on about some movie about to come out called *Jacob's Ladder*, how spooky it looks and how he plans to sneak into the R-rated flick, I'm watching, waiting for the bad thing to happen.

But it's business as usual: chatter and laughter of other kids, a few obnoxious boys trying to get the attention of girls by acting stupid, and assholes being assholes, shooting spitballs while yucking it up.

But nothing unusual.

And the humming continues.

It never lasts this long. It never warns me this far in advance. Usually, it's a few seconds, maybe a few minutes before the bad thing happens. This time it feels endless, and my head is throbbing.

No. I thought I outgrew these.

Suddenly, as if on cue, the lights feel like they've been cranked a million watts. My eyes are burning.

I close them, putting my head on the table.

"Hey, man, you okay?" Timmy asks.

I start to tell him that it's only a headache, but the pain is immediate, violent, and sharp. A blade shoved into my brain.

I cry out.

Though my eyes are closed, I feel a change in the atmosphere.

I know that people are looking at me.

I remember in fifth grade when a particularly nasty migraine hurt so bad that I cried in class.

Everyone laughed.

Now, two years later, an age when boys aren't supposed to cry, I know I'll be mercilessly teased.

The humming is now a hissing, rising in pitch. And, there's another sound. *Many* sounds, like a detuned radio rising in volume.

I need to get up and away, head to the bathroom where I can ride this out in private.

I get up and open my eyes.

A blast of pain forces them shut.

There's a chorus of laughter around me.

Timmy is right at my side. "Hey, need me to get someone?"

I stumble forward blindly, bumping into chairs.

More laughter.

The hissing gets louder, drowning everything else. But

it's not just hissing or humming now. It's voices. Music. Strange electronic beeping. Other sounds that I can't even recognize, as if someone had tuned into every radio, TV set, computer, car radio, CB, and any other device that transmits signals, and opened a direct line into my head, cranked them all to ten, in one swelling cacophonic wall of pain.

And it *hurts*.

I've never heard anything like this. At worst, I might overhear a few people thinking at once, and it gets confusing. But this is like someone tuned into every signal in a twenty-mile radius and blasted it straight into my head.

I bump into more objects. Chairs, tables, or other people. I don't know. My sense of touch and place are overwhelmed by the clamor.

I hit something hard and fall to the ground.

I cry out.

The pain gets worse.

Much worse.

I scream, only to hear something other than the reverb racing through my head.

But I can't even hear my own scream.

In the past my migraines were short-lived, lasting from twenty minutes to a couple of hours.

I don't think I can survive another five minutes of this one.

And yet, the sound and pain, somehow, increase exponentially, so loud I can no longer make out any of the sounds — a digital tsunami threatening to deafen me, or make my head explode.

I'm covering my hands over my ears, fetal on the ground, crying, shuddering.

Something wet and sticky trickles between my fingers.

Blood.

My entire body is burning as if the liquid inside me is boiling.

There's a building pressure as if I'm going to explode.

The noise continues to grow louder.

Pain increases.

More blood from my ears.

I need it to end.

I'd even accept the crushing blow of one of my bullies' boots against my skull if that meant ending the pain.

I feel something else I've never felt — a *clicking*.

My body straightens in one spastic stretch as if someone pulled on either end of me and violently snapped me.

My eyes shoot open.

I scream.

And then, somewhere in the distance, an explosion.

Followed by darkness.

The only sound I can hear is the piercing whistle of my ruptured eardrums.

But every other sound is gone.

And the pain is only a ghost in my skull and bones.

I stand in confusion.

As my eyes adjust to the natural light bleeding through the ceiling's few windows, I see that every eye is upon me.

And they're *all* afraid.

Chapter Two

Ben Shepherd Age 12

~

I'M SITTING in the backseat as my aunt Trudy drives me home.

We drive in silence.

Which is just as well, since I'm still trying to process what happened.

I want to think that what my teacher told Trudy is the truth: I got a horrible migraine which just so happened to occur at the same time as a power outage that knocked out half the town.

I'd love to think that I'm not the one responsible.

But I know better.

This was me, and I know it as sure as I know my name.

I don't know *how* or *why*, but I did this. And I'm pretty sure that the kids know I did it, too.

My life in this school will never be the same. Kids will

make fun of me even more, calling me a freak, or whatever funny derogative nickname they can conjure.

I want to cry, but hold it in.

I can't stand the thought of Trudy seeing me crying.

I already feel like she doesn't like me. That the only reason she looks after me on days my dad is out of town or working late is because she feels so sad that my mother, her sister, died from a stroke a few years ago.

I see her looking at me in the rearview.

"You sure you're okay? I can take you to the walk-in clinic."

"I'm fine. I just need some rest," I say.

"Are you sure? I think you should see someone, at least to rule out anything worse."

Worse? I can't imagine worse than what I just went through. If there's worse, I don't ever want to feel it.

But I can't tell Trudy what really happened. She has no idea that my dad and I are special.

And the last thing I want is some doctor examining me. What if they find something abnormal, something that tells them about my gift, or *gifts*?

On the rare occasion that I do need to see a doctor, Dad takes me to ones that he's already screened. Ones who work with people like us, and have a deal with the government to keep our secret.

So, no, Aunt Trudy, a walk-in clinic will *not* work.

It was weird enough to try and explain to the nurse that my eardrums were fine, even though they'd ruptured and blood was spilling from them just ten minutes before. Heck, I don't even know how that happened. I've always healed fast, but not *that* fast. I didn't feel any pain in my ears, and I'm sure that's not normal.

We pull onto our street.

"Want to go to my house or yours?"

Either way, she's coming with me. If I go home, I can head up to my room and pretend to sleep. If I go to her house, she'll want me to sit in the living room with her. That's always awkward. Usually, I'll read or do homework while she sits and watches TV. She hasn't worked in years, living off an inheritance from her mother along with a few smart real estate investments. She spends most of her time either watching TV or hitting the gym. But if the power's out at her house, then we'll be forced to talk.

"My house, please."

"Okay," she says.

IT'S BEEN five and a half hours since we came home and one hour since the power came back on. I'm lying in bed reading *The Talisman* by Stephen King, trying not to think about what my father will say when he gets home.

I hear the door open behind me.

I turn around to see Dad standing there in his black suit and pants, his face serious like he knows more than whatever the nurse told Aunt Trudy. "What happened?"

I'm not sure how to tell him.

He's lectured me countless times, whenever we moved to a new place, warning me how important it is that I never tell anyone about my gift.

"If you see something's about to happen, make sure you're safe, but do not intervene. Ever."

Most people don't know that our kind exist. It would mean big problems for us if they did, not to mention the secret government program my father works for.

I can't imagine how he's going to react when he learns that seeing things isn't my only gift. And that I allowed so many witnesses to see me.

I hedge around it, talking about my migraines, but he rolls his finger: *get to the point.*

Does he already know?

If so, the buildup will only anger him. My father, John Shepherd, isn't exactly known for his patience.

"I think I caused the power outage."

He sits on the edge of my bed. "Why do you think that?"

I'm struggling not to get emotional. Dad doesn't like tears. He doesn't know how to deal with them. He says they make you weak, and that the weak are easy prey.

"Because I could feel it building inside me," I tell him about the humming, how it was similar to when something bad is about to happen, but this time it was different. I explain it all: the immense pain, the building pressure, and the explosion inside me that happened at the same moment as the power went out.

He's staring at me. I can't read his expression. He looks like he's trying to decipher a foreign language printed on my skin.

"Is this the first time this has happened?"

"Yes, sir."

"Can you do it again?"

"*Again?* I don't ever want to feel something like that. Ever."

"What were you feeling before this happened?"

"Nothing."

"Nothing? You weren't feeling *anything*? You were just mindlessly wandering the cafeteria?"

I tell him about what happened with Rick — the bully at the bus stop. I tell him how I was worried that I might've messed things up for Timmy or me.

"What have I told you about getting into fights?"

"I can't just sit by and let him ridicule Timmy every day!"

"Has he ever hit Timmy?"

"He pushed him!"

"But did he hit him? Was Timmy *actually* attacked?"

"No."

"Then you don't need to get involved. If Timmy's not man enough to stand up for himself, that's *his* problem, not *yours*."

"So, I'm supposed to sit by and let a bully pick on my best friend?"

"Find new friends. Here, I'm going to make it easy for all of us: I forbid you from seeing Timmy anymore."

Dad stands and heads for the door.

"What?" I cry out. "Where is this coming from?"

Dad wasn't warm and cuddly, but he was rarely a jerk. *Why is he acting like this?*

Dad turns, gets in my face, and bores his blue eyes right into mine. "Rick is right, Timmy *is* a pussy, and I don't want my son hanging out with pussies."

I stand, feeling an energy ripple through me. Anger, mixed with something else.

And then I hear the hum.

No, not again.

I close my eyes.

Dad pushes me back onto the bed. "Ah, I see he's made you a pussy too."

I open my eyes, glaring at him. How can he talk like this to me? Why is he being such an asshole? A bully?

"What?" He smirks. "You going to do something, Ben?"

I don't get it. It's as if Dad is channeling one of the jerks in school. Like they jumped into his body and took control.

17

I don't like it.

The energy starts coursing through me.

My head is pounding.

I hear the broadcasts again, a chaotic mix of music, voices, and beeps. A static that grates like sandpaper against my rawest nerves.

The pressure is building, the sounds growing louder, though not piercing like before.

"Come on, Benny," Dad laughs. "*Do* something."

I hate when people call me Benny.

I stand back up and without even thinking, I shove him, hard.

As my hands touch him, I feel another, smaller explosion inside.

He stumbles backward, and my room falls into darkness.

The power is out.

The house is still.

My dad laughs as he goes to the window and opens the blinds to the darkness outside.

Not a single light in any of the houses for as far as we can see.

He turns and stares at me, eyes wide, a rare smile claiming his face.

He wasn't being mean. Dad was coaxing me to cause another power outage, to determine if I was truly capable of what I'd imagined.

"I think we've found your real gift."

"No, I don't want this." I shake my head. "I don't want *any* of these gifts!"

It was bad enough that I picked up on people's thoughts I didn't want, had visions that didn't help me and only made me anxious, but whatever this is, being overwhelmed and causing power outages, *this* is too much.

I turn and fall on my bed, punching the mattress, screaming.

I feel his hand on my shoulder, and think he's going to turn me around and lecture me on allowing my emotions to escape me.

But my father hugs me instead.

And despite my best efforts, I cry.

He pats my back as he holds me tight. "It's going to be okay, Ben."

I let years of pent up emotions flow free — years of feeling like a freak, of never having known my mother, years of not having friends or anyone to share my real feelings with.

It all comes out.

He holds me tighter, repeating, "It's going to be okay."

For the first time, I get the sense of a despair my father must've been feeling all this time, too. Raising a boy on his own, working at a job where his life was always in danger. Emotions were a luxury he couldn't indulge in, so he taught his son to be tough like him.

But now, as he holds me, I feel like he might be crying too.

I wonder if he's crying because he's happy to bond with me at this moment, or *sad*. Maybe he's been dreading this day for years, the moment I'd be doomed just like him by our curse.

He finally pulls away, but it's so dark in my room that I can't tell if his eyes are wet.

"There's a place that can help you."

"What place?"

"The school where I went. A place where you can be yourself. A place that will teach you to control your gifts."

Chapter Three

Ben Shepherd Age 12

~

TWO WEEKS LATER...
Anchor Harbor, Washington

~

WE'RE DRIVING up to the school in Anchor Harbor, about one hour north of where we live, and I'm doing my best not to be anxious. I try to find peace in the tall trees flanking the road as far as we can see.

Dad told me that the school is a great place. Private, and for "gifted" children. I asked why he never mentioned it before, and he said that my gifts weren't as pronounced before. As far as he'd known, I was only "slightly gifted." But now that he knows what I can do, the school will be eager to help me.

Between the lines, I see what he *really* means: now that

he sees the damage I can cause, the school is the *only* place that can help me.

"You went to this school?" I ask, even though I know.

"Yes. For six years. They helped me get my powers under control."

"What *are* your powers? Can you tell me now?"

He smiles, scratches the cleft in his chin, then says, *"Similar to yours. I'm a telepath. I see things. But, this electricity thing, I've never seen anything like it."*

Except when he says it, his mouth isn't moving.

I look at him confused.

Did you just talk into my head?

"Yes," he says, his mouth still not moving, *"I can communicate on another level."*

Can you read my mind?

I imagine all of the horrible thoughts over the years he might've been privy to, and my face feels hot. Then I think of the embarrassing ones.

Now he talks with his mouth. "Don't worry, Ben. I'm not *always* reading your mind. I give you your space."

"You can just turn it on and off?"

"Yes."

"And *that's* what you do for your job? They have you spying on people?"

"You know I can't go into details. But, yes."

"So, you're a spy? Cool!"

He smiles.

"Will I be able to do the same thing?"

"I'm not sure. That's what the school will help you figure out. Every Deviant is different, but some abilities run in families, with generational and other variations, of course."

"Deviant? There's a name for what we are?"

"One of many. But yes."

We drive in silence.

I stare out the window, seeing a deer and a fawn on the roadside ahead.

Dad starts to slow in case they jump in front of us.

Instead, the deer dart into the woods.

"How long do I have to live here?" I ask, trying to be strong.

"You're not living here. You'll come home on weekends and holidays. I'll also come up to see you whenever I'm able."

"But how long? You said you were here six years. I don't want to live here for *six years*."

"As long as it takes to get your gifts under control."

I turn my face back to the window. I'll cry if I don't.

At first, I was excited to meet other kids like me, and maybe finally fitting in. But that was before I knew it was a boarding school. It's not like I see my dad all that much during the week. He's always working late, and I spend more time with Aunt Trudy. But still, now we're a two-hour drive apart. The school may as well be in another state. And what if Dad has to move again for his job? For all I know, he could wind up in Florida next month, and weekend visits will be out of the question.

"What if I don't like it? Can I come home?"

Dad sighs. "You can't go to a regular school. Not until you can control yourself. It's just not safe. For you or the other kids."

"I wouldn't hurt anyone."

"I'm not saying you would, but you also don't know the full extent of your powers. What you've seen so far might be just the beginning."

Just the beginning?

I swallow.

"Will the headaches get worse? I'm not sure I can take that."

"They'll help you with that."

"Did you get headaches?"

"Sometimes. But I don't think they were as bad as yours."

"Great."

Another sigh. "Listen, Ben. There are two ways to roll with this. You can dwell on all the negatives: how things are going to change, how you won't be home, and how you won't see your old friends. Or you can choose to see the opportunities ahead: a chance to start over, a chance to be with other kids like you, a chance to determine your future. Like I said, ninety percent of life is interpretation."

I say nothing.

We're pulling up to a giant set of wrought iron gates. A black oval circle set in the concrete column to the right of the gates reads *The Academy for Talent and Distinction*.

There's a small guard's building in front. A man in uniform approaches my father's side of the car.

I note his holstered gun and wonder how many schools greet you at the gate with a weapon.

This place is going to suck.

Chapter Four

Ben Shepherd Age 12

I'm in line for the snack bar, eying the freshly baked cookies, thinking that so far, four days in, the school doesn't suck as much as I'd imagined.

It feels more like a vacation. My room, in one of the six dorms, is all mine. It has everything I could want — a bed, a bathroom with a shower, my own mini-fridge and microwave, a Nintendo and a small TV, along with a VCR and access to a library of movies, including some R-rated ones.

The campus is massive — more like a tiny village than a school. There are three in all: an elementary, a middle, and a high school, all ringed around a giant courtyard where kids mingle between classes and at night for social events.

I've yet to make any friends, let alone really talk to

anyone, but I'm still going through the orientation process, meeting with people who are giving me all sorts of tests, most of them medical and involving blood work, along with an endless battery of questions about my gifts.

I'm supposed to start classes next week, and I'm actually looking forward to it.

I take my cookie and carton of milk to the courtyard, looking for a place to sit that will give me a good view of others, without attracting attention. The circle is composed of gardens, gazebos, and cobblestone paths.

I stay along the outer edge, finding a bench in front of a corner created by two bordering hedgerows.

I sit with my back to the tall bushes, take a bite of the cookie, warm and oozing with buttery chocolate goodness, and look out across the courtyard.

It's three fifteen and students drift out of their classes still wearing their school uniforms: boys in blue pants with white shirts, girls in plaid skirts or blue pants with white shirts, some wearing navy sweaters with the school's crest embroidered over their hearts. Some kids are sitting on benches like me, drinking sodas or eating snacks. Others are playing hacky sack or Frisbee. A few of the artier kids are painting or drawing, and a girl with long black hair is playing a sad song on the violin.

I'm surprised that none of the kids are using their gifts. I'm not sure what I expected to see, maybe some kids playing football, one of them teleporting to catch a long pass while another shoots a fireball at the ball.

But there doesn't seem to be any magic here. The young teacher, Miss Marlena who took me on a tour and laid out the ground rules on Day One, told me that using one's powers outside the curriculum is frowned upon.

Some of the kids must ignore the rules, *right?*

It is a school, after all. And what's a school without the class clowns, rule breakers, and boundary pushers?

A kid in a cobalt blue jacket dives to catch a Frisbee, and before he hits the ground manages to flick his wrist and fire it back to the guy who threw it.

Impressive.

I keep eating the cookie, wishing I'd bought two. I wonder how Timmy is doing. My father let me call to tell him I was going to a private school, but wouldn't let me say anything more. Timmy asked if it had to do with the power outages. I hated not being able to tell him the truth, but I lied, saying no, it was some academy my father had gone to, which was nearly impossible to get into, and a position had recently opened.

I'm not sure if Timmy bought it, but like a good friend, he read between the lines and didn't press the issue.

"Will I see you anymore?"

"I'll be home on weekends, I think," I said. "Don't worry. You're not getting rid of me that easily."

"It's not going to be the same without you, Ben. But good luck."

Then he hung up, and I'm pretty sure he was crying.

I wonder if he's found another friend. Or if the bullies are picking on him even more now that I'm not there to intervene.

While my mind was wandering, my eyes settled across the courtyard, just past a group of girls sitting on a grassy spot, to the bench behind them, where a girl is sitting alone. She's wearing glasses and has super long red hair. She has a large book in her lap and is either writing or drawing — it's hard to tell from here.

I'm not sure why, but I can't look away.

It's not like she's so beautiful I can't help but stare. She may very well be, but I'm too far to know something like that.

Her hand moves back and forth in a sweeping motion on her page. Yes, she's definitely drawing.

I continue watching as if she's on a well-lit stage and I'm alone in the darkened theater.

She looks up at me.

I quickly look down, grabbing my milk and taking a drink.

No, I wasn't staring at you. Not at all. Nope, not me.

I focus on the last bites of my cookie as if I'd never eat another, waiting for a chance to look up again. Too soon and she may still be watching.

I count to sixty, using Mississippi to make it proper in my head. Then I look up.

But she's not on the bench.

And I panic.

I need to see her again, and I don't know why.

It's like she's some long lost friend I was searching for in a crowd, and now I've finally found her, only to lose her again.

I stand up to get a better view of the courtyard, my eyes scanning the little clusters, and people walking the cobblestone path.

No sign of her.

A girl speaks from behind. "Looking for someone?"

I jump, dropping my milk.

A hand reaches out, grabbing it fast enough to amaze me.

I turn and see her, the redheaded girl.

She smiles. "Hi."

And I stare, dumbly, unable to form any words. Unable to think of anything other than how utterly beautiful she is.

But I can't *say that*. Not *to her!*

She's my height, slim, with skin like porcelain. Unlike most of the girls I've seen so far, she's wearing a long blue cotton dress, to match a sky colored sweater. Her eyes are bright green, her lips full and pouty.

Pouty lips? When the hell have I ever noticed a girl's pouty lips?

My heart is racing. My thoughts are a jumbled mess. And she's staring at me.

I can't move.

I'm standing here, speechless.

What the hell is going on?

Why is she staring at me?

Then I remember that she said *Hi* and that most *normal humans* expect a response.

"Hi!" I shout.

What the hell? Why am I shouting?

My heart is racing.

She laughs.

Is she laughing at me?

Oh, God. I must look like such a dork, like I've never talked to a girl before or something.

I *have* talked to girls. Many, in fact. No, I've never dated any, but I've had crushes on at least six, and never have I ever felt so paralyzed.

"You're new here, right?" She offers her hand. "I'm Willow Fairchild."

Willow Fairchild?

Her name sounds like a fairytale.

I reach out to shake her hand. Mine is trembling.

Why?

Our hands grasp.

Hers is so warm.

I squeeze her palm and pump, like I'm shaking hands with a friend's father, rather than a girl.

"Ben. Ben Shepherd."

"Nice to meet you, Ben."

She looks down at my bench. "Can I sit with you?"

"Um, okay."

I brush away stray crumbs, wondering why on earth she's come over to sit with me. Did she see me staring? Is she here to tell me to stop or she'll report me?

She slides out of her backpack, drops it softly on the ground beside the bench, then takes a seat.

I sit, about as far from her on the bench as possible, leaving about three feet between us.

She looks down at the space between us, then up at me. "I don't bite."

She laughs, and it's beautiful music.

I still don't know why she's here.

"Sorry," I say, scooting closer.

She looks down at the space between us again, now about a foot. "Woah, not so close, Romeo!"

My face burns as I scoot back over.

She laughs again.

Now I'm sure she's probably some popular girl coming to rile the new kid.

I hate her.

She puts her hand on mine. "Relax, Ben. I'm just playing with you."

Her eyes lock on mine, and it's impossible to hate her.

Her hand is still on mine. Like, way too long.

I want to pull away, but I'm not sure what she'll do. If she'll take offense, or call it out and fake scold me.

This girl has me twisted and turned twelve ways from Tuesday.

Her hand is still on mine.

This is officially the longest any girl has ever touched me.

She's still staring at me with eyes that bore into my soul.

"You're cute when you're nervous."

"I'm not nervous," I say, yanking my hand back.

"No, of course not," she says, sarcastically.

"What's your problem? Did you come over here just to mess with me?"

"No. Not *just* to mess with you."

She's smiling. I'm not sure if I love her smile or loathe it.

There's something about her, a confidence that belies her appearance. I thought she was a quiet, artistic girl, maybe shy like me. Someone I might share some things in common with.

But she isn't.

"Then why are you here?"

"Because if I didn't come over, you would've just sat here on the bench staring at me forever."

"Stare at you? Um, you must have me confused with someone else."

I turn away like I'm going to get up and leave, but I'm only trying to hide my reddening face.

"What's your power?"

"Power?" I turn back to her, hoping the redness has faded.

"You can tell me. I won't tell anyone."

"I don't have *powers*. I'm not some superhero."

"Okay," she rolls her eyes. "What do you call whatever it is you have then?"

"Gifts."

"Oh, excuse me." She laughs. "Because *gifts* sound so much better than powers."

Now I do want to get up.

I've never met a girl bully. And I don't know how to

handle her. It's not like I'm going to tell her to fuck off or something.

I've never had a problem speaking up for myself when boys picked on me. In a way, I enjoyed proving them wrong. They thought they were toying with a weakling — they never counted on my being able to take care of myself.

But I won't fight a girl.

Hell, I'm still not even sure she's being mean. Maybe this is her way of flirting.

"If this is your way of flirting, you suck at it," I say.

Her eyes widen.

And for a moment, I think that maybe I went too far.

Then her smile returns. But this time it's different. A knowing smile, like now we're speaking the same language.

"*There's* the Ben Shepherd I was hoping to meet."

"You say that like you've heard of me."

"Not heard of so much as dreamed of."

"You *dreamed* of me?"

"Many, many times."

I'm not sure if she's still hazing me. Her eyes are more serious than before.

"How many times?"

"Since I was seven. And I'm thirteen now."

"You've been dreaming of me since you were *seven?*"

"It's my *gift*. I see things."

"What did you dream? Like you just saw me in your dreams, or you dreamed we were going to meet in the future?"

"You still haven't told me *your gift*."

I look around, to make sure that no one else is in earshot. I'm not sure why I'm so secretive. I'm in a school where everyone has a freaky ability. I guess old habits die hard.

"Sometimes I sense things that are going to happen."

"Tell me more."

I try to explain as best I can, and tell her how much I hate it because I never actually know what's going to happen. "It's such a useless gift!"

"Be glad you don't know. It's worse to know exactly what's going to happen and not be able to stop it."

"So you dream the future?"

"Yes," she said.

"And you dreamed of me?"

She nods.

"That we'd meet?"

"And much much more."

"What does that mean?"

She smiles. "I can't tell you."

"Why not?"

"Maybe the same reason you didn't tell me about your other gift?"

"What other gift?" I ask, knowing full well that I'm doing an awful job at pretending.

She stands then bends over to get her backpack. "Come and find me when you're ready to be honest."

"Sorry," I say, "but I'm new here, and I've only just met you. I don't know who I can trust."

"You can trust me, Ben."

I nod. "Do *you* know my other power?"

"I know of many other powers."

"Many? I only know of two, maybe three." The way I see it is I have three crappy *powers*: I have visions, I can sometimes pick up people's thoughts, and apparently, I also have freakouts that can cause power outages.

"You'll have many more than three," she says with a knowing smile.

A beeping interrupts her.

She looks down at her right hand. "Ah, time to go."

"When will I see you again?" I ask, like a desperate loser who can't stand for this moment to end.

"Tomorrow. Same place. Same time."

She unzips her bag and pulls out a big black art journal; I think the same one she was drawing in when I saw her across the courtyard.

"Here," she says, handing it to me.

"What is it?"

"Some of my dreams," she says, zipping her bag. "Goodbye, Ben Shepherd."

"Goodbye, Willow Fairchild," I say.

Once she's out of sight, I sit back down on the bench and open the book to the first pages.

The very first page reads: FOR BEN.

A tingle thrills me as I turn the page.

And there, spread out over two pages, in charcoal, is a drawing of me as a six-year-old, sitting at my desk in first grade, crying because the light was hurting my eyes.

What the hell?

I turn the page, and this time it shows my father and me at my mother's tombstone, placing flowers.

My heart is racing again.

Did she dream these moments?

What else has she seen?

I turn the pages and find more of my life. She drew the time I was looking for my cat who ran away and the time I beat up Jack Graves for making fun of my mom being dead. She drew the time my dad was in the special hospital with a gunshot wound and Aunt Trudy brought me to see him. The last filled-in page has a drawing of me in the fetal position crying on the cafeteria floor just before my third "gift" revealed itself.

I stare at the page as if it were a window into my past,

wondering what else does this girl know about me, or my future?

The next few pages are blank, and I figure that's it. But then, many pages later, I find one last drawing.

A girl is reaching up to touch a black, fuzzy star.

And though it makes no sense, I'm chilled to the bone.

Chapter Five

Ben Shepherd Age 15

~

"TRY AGAIN," Mr. Kotke says, standing in front of my workstation, his eyes narrowing on me.

The computer lab is empty except for us. The lights are off, so I can better focus on the screen and the empty file folder which reads FILLME.

I try to ignore my teacher's intense stare, made all the more severe by a mop of shock-white hair hanging over his eyes. He looks less like a mid-thirties teacher than some trendy fashion mogul or Parisian director, always in black pants and a black long-sleeve shirt. Today's tie is orange, matching his glasses.

The tie *always* matches the glasses.

"Are you focusing?" he asks, frustrated.

"Yes," I lie. The truth is, it's hard to focus on the same thing for an hour straight every weekday for a month. I'm starting to doubt that I'm as capable as he thinks I am.

Perhaps my power is limited to telepathic communication with electronics. I can perform basic functions on computers, turn devices on and off. I can execute programs, basically, do anything I could do with my hands, a mouse and a keyboard, except I'm only using my mind.

But what he's asking me to do now, I don't even think it's technically possible, let alone feasible for me.

"You just need to fill it with something."

"I don't know how!"

"Stop thinking of how, and get it done."

"How do you do something if you don't know how?"

"We've gone over this a hundred times, Ben. You're getting caught up in your knowledge, and that will limit you. Don't consider if it's possible. Be like Nike and just do it."

I laugh.

Kotke comes around to my side of the table and sits beside me.

Despite his eccentric style, he's serious when he talks. "When you shut down your city's power station did you know how to do it? Did you have a working knowledge of how to overload the grid or shut down the station?"

"No."

"Right! You just did it."

"I wasn't trying to do it, though. I was reacting to a lot of pain, and it *just happened*."

Kotke nods. "What about the things you can do now? You can turn on the lights when you enter a room without touching a thing, yet I'm guessing you don't know how to bypass the switch. Correct?"

I sigh. "Correct."

"So how do you do that?"

"I don't. If I want the lights on. I think them on. But I don't know *how* I do it."

"Okay. Let's pretend this computer is your girlfriend. You want to tell Willow a story. Go ahead. Tell her a story. *Any story*. But don't speak. Think it instead."

"I don't have any stories."

"*Everyone* has stories, Ben."

I stare at the computer again, picturing myself talking to Willow.

She's not really my girlfriend. I haven't even kissed her. But I don't correct Mr. Kotke. I'm not sure why, but I like people thinking that we're going out, even though I never say that we are.

It's a weird relationship. It's like we're dating in so many ways, but without any of the romance. We're always hanging out. We call each other every night before going to bed in our dorms. And the rare weekends when we don't go home are spent together. And she's always hugging on me or cozying up next to me on the couch. She even says "love 'ya" at the end of every call. It's not "I love you," but it must mean something. She's not this close to anyone else.

And it's not like she doesn't know how I feel. I told Willow that I liked her six months into our friendship. But she said it's best we don't date because she'll only break my heart.

I should move on. But whenever I try to spend time away from Willow, to give her some space, she comes around even more. It's like she doesn't want to date me while wanting to spend every waking moment together. And she doesn't want me to date anyone else.

I think she wants to be with me, but something is stopping her.

What that something is, I don't know.

I turn my attention to the computer screen.

Okay, you want a story, here's your story.

I used to have a friend named Timmy. One of the nicest guys you would ever want to meet. Unfortunately, Timmy was also overweight, and that made him stick out.

And the last thing you want to do as a kid in middle school is stick out.

Sticking out is like begging to get picked on. You may as well wear a shirt that says, "Pick on me, I'm different."

Timmy and I got along great.

I tried to give him some confidence. Told Timmy that he had to stick up for himself. I offered to teach him to fight. But Timmy wasn't a fighter. And he had zero interest in learning to defend himself.

Why? I'll never know.

He was a kind soul who figured it was better to take a few hits than turn to violence. Probably because he was scared that fighting back would only lead to more violence.

I had to leave Timmy behind to come here, a school that he would've loved. A school for misfits.

Unfortunately, he wasn't the "right kind" of a misfit.

I promised Timmy that even though I was leaving, I'd visit every weekend.

And I did — at first.

But soon Timmy and I stopped talking.

I don't even know how it happened. Maybe it was because we no longer had much in common. I didn't get to watch much TV or movies or even read comics anymore. Over time we drifted apart.

And on the rare occasions I did see him, Timmy seemed resentful that I got to leave our shitty little school in our shitty little town while he had to stay.

It became easier to ignore him than deal with the guilt trips. I don't need to be made to feel bad every time we talk because "I've changed."

So I stopped returning his calls.

Stopped visiting.

And then, about a year and a half after I left for The Academy for Talent and Distinction, I got the news. Timmy could no longer take the bullying and loneliness.

He killed himself.

And unlike his other guilt trips, this one will hurt forever.

How's that for a story, Mr. Kotke?

I wipe the tears from my eyes and stand. "I need to use the restroom."

I finish up, go to the closest restroom, wash my hands, then splash cold water on my face to snap myself out of my funk.

My watch says I have five minutes left before my next class. Good. Just enough time to find out that I failed yet again.

At least there won't be enough time for another of these tests today.

I'm counting the minutes until I can head to lunch and meet Willow. She always knows how to get me out of these dark moods.

I return to his class and open the door to see Mr. Kotke sitting in my chair, smiling wide.

"What is it?"

"Come here!" he says pulling out the chair next to mine.

I sit.

He opens the folder that said FILLME.

Inside is a .wav file.

He presses play.

And, *somehow*, my voice says, "Okay, you want a story, here's your story. I used to have a friend named Timmy ..."

My voice continues to narrate. Kotke is practically bursting with joy.

"You did it, Ben. You actually did it."

Chapter Six

Ben Shepherd Age 17

〜

DAD and I are driving to Willow's house for Thanksgiving dinner.

This is the first time I'm meeting her father, Arnold Fairchild, who just so happens also to be my father's boss at Advanced Dynamics.

"So, this thing with Willow? How serious is it?" Dad asks.

"We're just friends."

"*Just* friends?"

I look over at him to see if he's teasing me, but he's not smiling in the way he has in the past when I've crushed on a girl.

"Yeah, just friends. Why?"

"No reason," he says, but I can tell he's lying.

Something's off, and I'm not sure what it is. Dad's been distant ever since I came home from school on Tuesday. I don't think he's mad at me. Maybe it has something to do with work. I wonder if he would've preferred that I stay in school over Thanksgiving break. He's been working more and more on weekends lately, always having some reason about "last minute developments" or some other excuse why I can't come home.

I used to mind, but nowadays, I'd rather spend time with Willow anyway.

Still, that doesn't mean I'm not offended.

But as I look at him, I can feel waves of boiling distress just under the surface. Maybe work is going bad. Maybe he's even in danger.

"What's wrong, Dad?"

"Nothing," he says, not moving his eyes from the road.

"Yes, there is. I can tell."

He looks at me. His face relaxes, but only a little.

"Yeah, you breaking into my mind now?"

I should tread carefully since he can definitely read me. He's probably doing it right now to see what I know, or think I know. He probably knows I'm lying about Willow, and that I'm absolutely in love with her, even if it's unrequited.

Shit.

Stop thinking about her.

He'll pick up on it!

Dad turns his attention back to the road as we drive through a winding, hilly area where the uber-wealthy live in their perfectly-sculpted estates. Most have walls or gates to keep out the riffraff. I laugh to myself at the arrogance one must have to think a gate or wall would keep out anyone truly determined.

It's weird; even though our school is the kind that rich kids would normally attend, I think most of the kids there are like me: middle-class or even poor. But unlike regular schools, wealth hasn't divided us. Rich kids hang with the poor, and nobody gets worked up about such trivial things. It's probably because we're all marginalized by our gifts—freaks at home, but the same at school. Of course there are still cliques. It is the real world, after all.

But on break, driving past the giant houses on hilltops, I can't help but feel like I don't belong here. Can't help but see the disparity between Willow and me.

And without even meaning to, I say, "I like her. A lot. But she says we should just be friends."

He looks at me and gives me one of his most compassionate smiles. "It's always good to have friends."

I sigh. "I don't want her as a *friend*. I want her to be my *girlfriend*."

"What's the rush? You're seventeen. You have your whole life ahead of you. Don't worry. If Willow doesn't like you in the same way, you'll meet someone who does. I guarantee it."

"I don't want anyone else."

I stare out the window as we pass a giant mansion that looks more like a hotel. All that house can't possibly belong to one family, can it?

"Do you think she doesn't like me because I'm not rich?"

"I doubt it, son."

"Then why? We're like best friends. We're into a lot of the same things. We get along great and make each other laugh. Sure, I'm not Fabio, but I don't think I'm hideous."

"No, son, you're not hideous."

"Thanks, Dad," I say sarcastically.

"I mean you're good looking. Any girl would be lucky to date you."

"So, what is it then?"

"Not everyone is lucky enough to know what they want

when they're young. Hell, when I was your age, I was still scared of girls."

"What about mom?"

"I didn't meet your mom until we were both in our twenties. She'd already dated a few jerks that taught her what *not* to go for in a guy, and I had gone out with some beautiful girls without much substance, enough to know what I didn't want in a wife."

"So, you're saying girls my age like jerks?"

"Not all of them, no."

"Should I act like a jerk?"

"God no. Be yourself, son. Don't ever act like someone you're not for a girl. You might get her to go out with you, but eventually, you'll get tired of acting. Then you'll realize that she doesn't love you because she doesn't even know you. I'd rather be with someone who appreciates me for exactly who I am than try to fit into some ideal which will surely change over time, anyway. It's always better to be authentic. A woman will appreciate that."

I stew on that for a while as we get closer to the Fairchild's house.

I suppose Dad is right. And though I hadn't planned it that way, I have been authentic with Willow. Maybe in time she'll come to appreciate that.

"Do you think I should wait for her, or date someone else?"

Dad laughs.

"What?"

"Sorry, Ben. It's just weird to be talking about dating with you. It seems like only yesterday you were sitting on my lap while I read you bedtime stories."

His voice cracks, just a little. I'm close to whatever pain he's feeling. The thing he won't talk about.

Does it have to do with me? Nostalgia for the past?

Maybe he misses Mom. She's been dead for seventeen years, and as far as I know, he's never dated anyone else.

Or maybe he is, and maybe she broke his heart?

I want to ask him, but how?

Then it's too late.

We've arrived at Willow's, a giant mansion atop a hill taller than every other in town.

I feel insignificant as we begin our ascent up the steep driveway.

THE FAIRCHILD'S dining room is sprawling, as is the table which holds nearly thirty people. Every seat is full, with a bunch of Dad's co-workers from Advanced Dynamic; the Academy's principal, Ms. Sutter; my computer teacher, Mr. Kotke, and a few other teachers and school staffers I don't know by name, but always see around the halls.

Willow and I are the only young people at the table, sitting next to one another, trading whispers and jokes while the adults talk and fill their mouths from the lavish displays of food. There are even servants on duty, seven of them. They shepherd dishes and constantly flowing drinks to the table.

"Your parents went all out for this dinner," I say.

"Well, their staff did, yes," Willow corrects me. "Mom doesn't cook. Like, ever."

Mrs. Fairchild looks like an older version of Willow, but she lacks the purity of her daughter's smile. But she does smile a lot, especially as she tosses back glasses of wine, chatting with every soul at the table. She seems nice enough, but I sense a distance between her and Willow.

Her father, Arnold Fairchild, is a short man with graying hair that is starting to bald. But he's also the loudest, most confident man in the room, with a commanding presence, the person that everyone listens to either because he has the best stories, or because he pays them well.

He's the director of Advanced Dynamics, and AD works with our school. My father reports directly to him. But beyond that, I don't know a thing about him other than he has a *very* firm handshake, and keeps looking at me during dinner, which is slightly unnerving. I want to tell him, "Hey, relax. Your daughter doesn't even like me like that. You've got nothing to worry about, man."

For as well as I know Willow, she's always been tight-lipped about her family and changes the subject when I've asked about them. I figured they must be awful; but both her father and her mother are very personable, even if they seem a bit phony. Then again, I think most adults are fake in the way they always seem to talk around the things they really want to say.

Dad seems more relaxed now with a few drinks in his belly. There's a woman across from him named Diana. She's married to the man to her right, Gerald, but he's hardly paying attention to her, kissing Arnold Fairchild's ass most of the night, and leaving Diana to flirt with my father.

I wonder if anyone else can pick up on the exaggerated smile she has for him, or the way she curls her hair as she talks to him, or that sparkle in her eyes when he's talking to her.

I wonder if they're secretly dating.

Maybe that's some of the tension I sensed in him earlier?

He's doing an excellent job of ignoring — or pretending not to notice — her flirtations while joking good-naturedly with her and Gerald.

After everyone finishes their meal, I need to pee, but

nobody seems to be getting up from the table anytime soon. Not while drinks are flowing and dessert is on the way.

I lean over to Willow. "Where's your bathroom?"

"I'll show you," she says, pushing her chair back.

"I'm going to show Ben around the house," she says to her parents.

Her father looks at us, saying nothing, staring right through me.

Her mother smiles. "We'll be doing dessert in about fifteen minutes."

"Okay," Willow says as she takes my hand and pulls me behind her.

We pass her father as he's telling a story to the others, but I can feel his eyes on me as we pass.

No way do I look to see if I'm right.

We make it out of the dining room and I deeply exhale.

Willow turns to me, "What?"

I laugh, not meaning to be so obvious. "Your dad keeps staring a hole into me."

She laughs. "Oh, yeah, he's a little overprotective."

She leads me up the stairs past a knight in shining armor holding a massive sword. It looks like a museum piece.

"He's not going to put this on and kill me, is he?"

"You wouldn't be the first," Willow says.

"What?"

She laughs. "I'm joking! Relax, Ben."

She runs faster up the stairs, leading me past several doors, and then pushes one of them open to what must be her bedroom.

"Just through there," she says.

"Wow, you have your own bathroom?"

"Yeah," she says as if it's no big deal.

I make my way into her bathroom then close the door.

I sit on the toilet, just to make sure I don't get any pee on her floor.

As I sit, I hope I don't suddenly have to poop. The thought of having to push one out with her right on the other side of the door is mortifying.

Fortunately, I only piss.

I flush, then wash my hands, and open the door.

She's lying on her bed, staring up at her ceiling.

Her door is closed.

It's just us in her room.

Her father is going to murder me.

"Can you turn out the lights?" she asks.

"Huh?"

"I want to see if the stars still glow."

I see the plastic stars on her ceiling, then find the switch and flick it.

The room goes dark, save for moonlight bleeding through her second story windowed door, leading to a balcony.

The stars on her ceiling are barely visible.

She pats the bed. "Come here."

My stomach churns as I imagine her father's footsteps coming down the hall, pausing in front of her door, turning the knob, opening it to see us lying on her bed. Even though we're probably not going to do anything, we'll still look guilty as hell.

I wonder if she locked the door.

She pats the bed again.

I sit beside her.

"No," she says. "Lie down."

"Um, okay."

I lie beside her.

She's an inch away.

My heart is pounding so loud I'm sure she can hear it.

I've sat next to her hundreds of times in my dorm, in her dorm, in rec hall, in the theater we sometimes go to, but I have never lain down beside her.

"When I was six, I was scared of the dark. My Dad put these stickers up and got a black light. He told me that next time I'm scared to imagine that I'm on some distant planet in a galaxy far, far away."

"Did it work?"

"Usually, when I went to sleep. But my parents used to turn off the black light when they checked on me, so when I woke up in the middle of the night the room was pitch black, and I felt all alone again."

"And what did you do?"

"Sometimes I'd turn the light on. Other times, I'd lay here in the dark and tell myself that everything would be fine. If something bad were going to happen, I'd have dreamt it already."

I look up at the ceiling, trying to imagine how much bigger and deeper the darkness seemed to a six-year-old Willow. How endless the night and its horrors must have felt.

"And that usually worked. But it didn't stop me from wanting to climb into my parent's bed. Just so I wouldn't be alone."

Her hand brushes mine. Her fingers close.

"I don't want to be alone anymore, Ben."

She moves.

My heart is racing.

I think I might have a heart attack right here on her bed.

I see her, just barely in the moonlight, as her face moves closer to mine. "I don't want to be alone."

She kisses me.

Oh, my God! She's kissing me!

I don't know what to do.

I've never been kissed.

I feel her tongue push my lips open, and then it's inside my mouth.

It's so warm.

So ...

Her hands move over my chest.

And then my dick stands at full attention.

Oh, God. What if she brushes against it? She'll know I'm hard.

I start to shift, trying to angle my body away from her.

She pulls my hand onto her breasts, kisses me harder.

Then climbs on top of me, her crotch on top of mine.

No way she can't feel my boner.

She sits up, almost riding me missionary, except we're fully dressed.

My hands move from her chest to her hips as she grinds against me.

If she keeps doing this, I'll explode. And I'm not sure how the hell I'm gonna clean up a mess in my pants without her father, or mine, or hell, maybe everyone at dinner, taking notice.

Not sure if she's reading my mind, but Willow hops off as suddenly as she'd hopped on.

"Sorry," she says, sitting up, turning the light on.

She looks out the window.

I reach out and run my hand over her long red hair. I never would've reached out and stroked her hair before now. "Sorry for what?"

"Leading you on."

I'm confused. I don't say anything, not wanting to whisper the wrong thing. After all these years of loving Willow from afar, and to be so close to something, anything approaching intimacy, I don't want to mess up and end up back in the Friend Zone.

"I *do* like you," she says.

Now I'm almost positive she's reading my thoughts.

And I don't even care.

I think, *I don't like you. I love you.*

She turns, eyes wet with tears, and looks at me, surprised. "You do? Love me?"

"Yes. And I think you feel the same way."

I hope that I'm right. If I'm not, that was way too bold.

She sighs. "I do love you, Ben. I've loved you, if it's possible, from the first time we met. I feel like I've known you my entire life. In a way, I have."

I remember how she said she'd dreamed of me ever since she was a kid, probably as she slept in this very bed.

"Then what's the problem?" My voice cracks, ever so slightly, making me cringe.

"Because I know what's going to happen."

"What's going to happen? Is your dad gonna kill me?"

She laughs. "No, my Dad will come to love you like a son."

"Really?"

She smiles. "Yes, really. He thinks that you'll save me."

"Save you from what?"

She takes my hands in hers as she shifts to sit cross-legged across from me on the bed. "I don't know how. And I don't know what from, nor do I know the exact date, but I'm going to die when I'm twenty-five.

My heart skips a beat.

My stomach drops.

"No."

She nods. "That's why I didn't want to get close to you. I don't want to leave you behind."

"If you know you're going to die, maybe you can prevent it. Get tests for cancer and stuff."

"My father will be doing that, believe me. But some things you can't stop."

"You said he thinks *I* can save you?"

"Yes."

"How?"

She shakes her head. "He wants to upload me onto a computer. Well, sort of a computer."

"Upload you? Like your brain?"

"My soul."

"Is that even possible?"

"Not yet."

"But it will be?"

"It's part of the reason you're at the school, Ben. My father sees things, too. And he saw you shortly after I started seeing you. You're going to be capable of great things. Things that will change the world."

I feel like an animal in a zoo, watched by strangers. I wonder what she and her father saw me doing. Did they see me at my worst? Fighting with my father? Crying? *Masturbating?!* I feel so exposed.

None of that compares to the bomb that Willow just dropped — *that she's going to die.*

"Do your visions *always* come true?"

"I don't know, as I don't always know the people I see. But as far as I can tell, *yes*, they've all come true."

"Wait a second. You said your dad has visions too. Did he say that I actually save you? Or that I upload your soul to some computer?"

"He doesn't tell me exactly what he saw. He seems to think that if he can upload my soul to a computer, he can eventually transfer it to another body. Or maybe even back into mine."

The world just opened a big box of crazy, and none of the old rules apply. Who am I to say it can't happen? I have gifts, some I apparently don't even know about. And now I go to school with others who have bizarre powers right out of sci-fi comics.

Maybe I can save Willow.

We have to try at least.

An idea comes to me as I stare out her door and see a meteor streak by in the night sky.

I go to the door, open it, and step onto the balcony.

I look up and smile.

"Come here," I say.

WE'RE LYING on her roof, staring up at real stars, holding hands.

It's cold up here, and the wind is picking up, but I don't care because I'm with Willow.

"This is much better," she says.

"You should have your dad put in a skylight."

She laughs. "I should ask."

We talk more about her childhood, about mine, talking around the thing we want to discuss most — just like the adults downstairs.

"You think your mom is looking for us yet? Dessert was like forty minutes ago."

"I doubt it. She's entertaining the guests."

"How about your dad?"

"He probably has guards searching the grounds."

"Really?" I ask, sitting up, looking around.

"No, not really," she laughs. "Man, you *are* gullible."

She leans over and kisses me again.

Unlike that first passionate kiss with the darting tongue

and desperately exploring hands, this one is soft, sweet, and lingering.

As she pulls away, I find the nerve to say what I've been trying to find the words for.

"I think it's stupid that you don't want to be with me because you might die. Hell, anyone could die at any time. Nobody knows how long they have. So, what, we all stay lonely so no one gets hurt? Every relationship is an eventual heartbreak. But what's the alternative? To inoculate yourself with loneliness? I don't see how that's better."

She says nothing, but her crying eyes, trembling lips, and subtle nod tell me everything.

"I don't want you to die. And I'm willing to do anything your dad thinks I can do to stop it from happening. But if it is going to happen no matter what, then at least we can pack as much fun into these years as possible. If you're gonna go out, go out living life to the fullest!"

She kisses me again. And then she hugs me.

It feels good to have her arms around me and mine around her.

I don't ever want to let go.

Suddenly, lights come on downstairs illuminating a large wooden deck and pool area with a bar, several wooden chairs, a fire pit, and a handful of tables.

Our fathers are standing near the pool, her father lighting a cigar.

We freeze, hoping they don't look up and see us.

There's no way to climb down the roof and stay silent enough not to draw attention. We'll need to sit here until they go back inside.

Her father's cigar wafts up on the breeze. It's a pleasant scent. Probably an expensive cigar that costs more than our car.

"What the hell do you mean?" Dad says, his voice loud

and angry.

Uh-oh.

"What's happening?" Willow whispers, pulling herself closer to me.

"I dunno. Dad's been acting weird ever since I came home."

We continue to eavesdrop, but most of their conversation is lost beneath the howling wind.

Judging from Dad's posture and crossed arms, he's pissed. Meanwhile, Mr. Fairchild looks relaxed, despite my father's angry tone.

My dad's voice picks up, "We don't know that!"

Fairchild's demeanor doesn't change. He says something I can't hear, takes another puff of his cigar.

My father points at Mr. Fairchild, yelling something else I can't hear. And then he follows with, "I'm not signing off on this."

Her father's voice finally rises. His demeanor shifts to match my father's. "You will, or you can resign."

My father turns and walks away.

My jaw drops.

"Did he just quit?"

Willow shakes her head, "I dunno."

"I need to get downstairs, quick."

But I can't move until her father goes back inside.

He takes another puff on his cigar, then looks up at us.

I freeze.

Shit!

I can't tell if he can see us. There's a lot of lights shining down onto where he is, and we're in the dark, so maybe he can't. But it sure feels like he can.

He takes another puff, then strolls inside.

Willow and I scramble down from the roof, onto her balcony, into her bedroom, then out and down the stairs.

We pass several people congregating in the halls, many saying goodbyes.

I spot my father at the front door.

He sees me and waves a hand, mouthing, *Come on.*

I turn back to Willow, afraid of what's coming next if my father did quit his job. Will I have to leave the school? Will I ever see Willow again?

I don't want to leave, but my father is waiting.

"Bye," Willow says, squeezing my hand.

I make my way to the door, thankful that the adults are oblivious to me.

I'm almost there when Arnold Fairchild steps into my path, eyes boring into my skull. "Leaving without saying goodbye?"

"Goodbye, Mr. Fairchild," I say reaching out to shake his hand.

He grabs my hand with his oaken handshake. But this time, it's joined by something else. He's saying something, but his lips aren't moving.

"I'll see you soon, Ben."

I nod, not sure what to make of this, and quickly find my father outside.

I follow him to the car, wanting to ask what's wrong, what his fight with Mr. Fairchild was about. But how do I do it without revealing that Willow and I were spying?

He gets in the car.

I climb into the passenger's side.

He keys the ignition and peels out.

I look at him.

His eyes are staring at the road, burning with an internal fire.

"What's wrong, Dad?"

"Not now, son."

And we drive in silence.

Chapter Seven

Ben Shepherd Age 17

~

Two weeks later

~

WILLOW and I are laying in my dorm room bed waiting for Dad to pick me up for the weekend.

"I wish you didn't have to go," she says, "I'm going to be so lonely here without you."

"I'd stay if I could. But I think something's wrong with Dad."

We've talked about our fathers' Thanksgiving argument a few times in the weeks since it happened. But neither man has told us what the argument was about. Willow even went so far to ask her father outright, saying she'd overheard "something" downstairs. He said it was *work* business, not *her* business.

I haven't had the courage to ask my dad.

But I have asked what was wrong a number of times. He said it was "work stuff" and "nothing for you to worry about."

Then he tried to pretend that he wasn't bothered, but I could see through it and knew better than to argue.

Whatever it was, I'm guessing it wasn't going to mean an end to his job. Willow told me that she wouldn't let her father fire mine if it came to that. I thanked her but wasn't sure she could save my father from himself if he wanted to leave. He's stubborn as hell.

If Dad wanted me to come home this weekend, I figured it was best that I did — at the very least, I could get an idea of what was happening. Not that the knowledge would do me any good if he *did* decide to quit. What was I going to do? Talk him out of it?

Maybe not, but I wasn't going to allow him to take me away from Willow. Especially not since we've finally started dating.

In the two weeks since Thanksgiving, we've grown closer than ever. Despite the intensity of Thanksgiving night on her bed, we haven't done anything beyond kissing and some light touching above the clothes. I'm following her lead. I'd love to go all the way, but am content to take things slowly, enjoying the moments we have, while we have them.

I try not to think about her premonition that she'll die at twenty-five. We haven't discussed it again. Nor have I seen her father. I'm not sure if I could bring it up with him. Again, I'll follow her lead. I think a part of me is afraid to talk about it, as if that will make it more real, and ignoring it will somehow alter fate's plans.

She runs a finger over my cheek, staring at me. "I guess I'll just have to hang out with Nils."

I narrow my eyes, pretending to be angry. "You wouldn't."

Nils is a classmate who has had a crush on her for more than a year. He's captain of the debate team and an insufferable douchebag who happens to have superhuman strength. He could kick my ass if he wanted to — I've seen him do some impressive stuff in our field training exercises — but thankfully he's not like the jock assholes I once went to school with. He seems to have enough confidence not to pick fights with the guy Willow chose to date instead of him. For now, anyway.

She kisses me.

"Please stay," she whispers, her fingers tracing the hairs on the back of my neck. I feel a chill as she wraps one leg over me, smiling devilishly as if she's about to climb on top of me.

I want to stay here forever.

Suddenly, a knock.

The knob starts to turn, but the door is locked.

"Ben?" My father's voice.

"Hold on a sec," I say, hopping out of bed and pulling my tucked-in shirt out of my pants to hide my erection.

Willow starts to unbutton her shirt, exposing her cleavage.

"Stop," I whisper.

She smiles that same evil grin, pops another button.

I can practically feel my father breathing down my neck just outside the door. He'll think Willow and I were doing something. And the last thing I want to hear from my dad on the way home is "the sex talk."

"Come on," I say, motioning for Willow to close her shirt — maybe the only time I will ever ask a girl to cover her breasts.

She buttons up, moves off the bed, and takes a seat at the desk.

I give myself a once-over in the mirror just to make sure there's no tell-tale sign of Willow and me making out. At least I no longer have to worry about my shirt hiding my arousal. A father's knock will kill it.

I open the door and meet his eyes. He'll suspect us if I don't.

But as I see him standing there with red eyes and pale skin, his hair a mess, shirt and pants both crumpled, I'm no longer worried that he'll pick up on something with *me*.

He looks like he's seen a graveyard breathing.

"Come on, son. We've got to go." Then he turns and leaves without even saying hi to Willow.

We exchange worried glances. Her eyebrows arch.

"Call me when you get home."

I nod, unable to say a word.

I kiss her, grab my backpack, and follow my father.

I have a horrible feeling about this weekend.

I FOLLOW Dad to the parking lot.

We get into his car.

The sky is gray overhead, threatening rain.

He looks nervously around as he pulls out of the driveway, then keeps checking the rearview as he navigates away from the school.

I don't say a word until I see that he's not getting on the highway like usual. He's driving along the main street, passing shops and gas stations, his eyes constantly on the rearview.

Rain begins to fall, hard.

"Where are we going?"

"Change of plans, son. We're going on a trip."

He pulls into a gas station, parks in the rear, and shuts off the windshield wipers while leaving his lights on.

"What's going on? Are you okay?"

He looks at me, his brow knitted in. He says nothing, like he's trying to find words.

A white van pulls up beside us, its windows tinted darkly enough that I can't see inside.

I lean forward in the passenger seat, my heart already out of control.

That bad feeling is getting worse. It's not psychic bad, nor am I getting a horrible migraine, but the fear is equally raw.

The van door opens.

A skinny black man in jeans and a black sweater gets out. A knitted hat covers most of his face, except for his eyes.

"Who is that?"

"A friend. Get out." Then Dad opens his door and climbs out of the car.

I follow, grabbing my backpack from the floor.

Dad says something to the man, hands him an envelope.

The guy looks at me, nods, then climbs into Dad's car and drives away.

What the hell is happening?

Dad goes toward the van's open driver's side, then looks back at me. "Get in."

I run around to the passenger side, open the door, and look inside.

I see several duffels and suitcases inside the van.

"What's going on, Dad?"

"We're leaving."

"Leaving where?"

"The country. Now get in."

I climb in, my heart racing, mind swirling in a chaotic vortex as I try to grasp onto any sense of what might be happening, desperate for something, *anything*, to make sense.

Dad starts driving, toward the highway, pulling onto the southbound on-ramp instead of heading northbound.

I wait for him to say something, to offer any explanation. But he just keeps driving, checking the side mirrors.

Finally, as we merge onto the highway, I have to ask, "What do you mean we're *leaving the country?*"

"We're going to Mexico."

"What? Mexico? We don't even know anyone in Mexico! Why are we going to Mexico?"

"Because they'll kill us if we don't."

I think he's joking at first. This *must* be some sort of prank. Dad's not exactly a pranking type, but it's the only thing that makes any sense — even if it's out of character.

But then he looks at me, his eyes wide and crazed, and I can tell that he isn't joking. Something is happening — or he *thinks* something is. He's in full panic mode. I've never seen him like this, not even close, and it's scaring the hell out of me.

"What are you talking about, Dad? *Who's* going to kill us?"

"The less you know, the better. Just in case."

"In case of what?"

He looks at me like he's about to say something.

But then there's a flash in front of us.

Dad swerves, barely missing a truck merging into our lane.

Copper floods my mouth.

I grab the handle to my right and cling for dear life.

I'm certain that the van will hydroplane into the center median, but somehow dad manages to regain control, swerving into the left lane and righting the van.

I swallow.

Dad stares out the windshield, his eyes bulging. "I need to focus on the road. I'll tell you more later."

I lean back in the seat, catching my breath, waiting for my heartbeat to slow. But I can't let go of the handle.

I WAKE up to the unfamiliar darkness of our motel room. The AC is cranked to full blast, so the sound drowns the highway. It worked well enough that we were able to fall asleep, but it's like a freezer in here now.

The clock on the nightstand next to my table reads 1:10 AM. We didn't get to bed until nearly midnight. I'm not even sure what state we're in.

We drove for what felt like forever, my father barely saying a word. Even when we stopped for fuel, to use restrooms, or grab a bite — all paid for with cash — he barely spoke.

He's seemed distracted all day, and afraid.

I thought about calling Willow from a pay phone, but I don't have change, and can't make a call without being seen. He's already said that we can't trust anyone.

This must have something to do with his job. Maybe whatever started boiling over on Thanksgiving has finally exploded.

What did my father do?

What could possibly require us to run?

Did he break the law?

Are we on the run from AD or the law?

I know that his job involves working with law enforcement in some way, which only confuses me further.

I look over in the darkness to the bed next to mine, but it's empty.

A light beneath the bathroom door tells me where he is.

I pull the covers tighter over my body, but the blanket is thin.

I get up, walk to the mirrored closet, and pull it open to see if there are any extra blankets inside. I see another two pillows, an iron and an ironing board, but no blankets.

I slide the closet door shut just as the bathroom door opens.

I squint into the light.

Dad steps out of the bathroom, dressed in his pants, shirt, and jacket. He barely looks at me as he walks over to his bed and sits.

He picks up the phone.

"Hey, if you're calling the front office, could you get another blanket or two?"

He says nothing, waiting for someone to answer.

I go into the bathroom, close the door, and sit on the toilet to pee. I'm too tired to stand *and* aim well.

Dad finally gets a hold of whoever he's calling. The walls are so thin I can hear him fairly well.

"Hello. My name is John Shepherd, and I'd like to turn myself into the sheriff's office for murder."

Murder?

What?

I can't hear anything else.

I finish peeing, pull up my boxers, open the door, and look at him.

The phone is in the receiver.

He's just sitting there, staring at the curtains.

I go over to him. "What's going on?"

He's not looking at me. More *through* me.

And still, he says nothing.

Instead, he stands, goes to the window, and opens the curtains to the motel lot. Lights flicker outside our window.

He returns to the bed, sits, folds his hands in his lap, and smiles while waiting patiently for the deputies to arrive.

"Dad! What's happening? What murder are you talking about?"

I want to shake him out of that smile. How can he just sit here when deputies are about to storm the motel?

He finally looks at me, giving me this Joker's smile I've never seen on him before. "I did bad things, son. It's best you don't know."

"What bad things?" I ask, feeling anxious while time keeps bleeding. The deputies will be here any moment. We need to leave, not sit here and wait.

"It's best you don't know. It's best you remember me well, son."

The way he looks at me when he says "son" sends chills through me. It's like he's not even in there. As though he's talking to a stranger. My dad has flipped the eff out!

"Dad, talk to me," I say, going over to him, "what did you do?"

He looks up at me, moving in a weird, dream-like slow motion as he eyes me up and down.

Please let this be a dream!

He shakes his head. "Go back to sleep. Everything will work itself out."

"What about going to Mexico? What about not trusting anyone?"

He smiles, waves his hand dismissively. "Forget all that. I was wrong. I need to set things right."

"What does that even mean? If you killed someone, you'll go to prison. I'll never see you again!"

I start bawling.

Even though I didn't want to go on the run, especially if that meant leaving school and Willow, I don't want my father in prison. I'd gladly go on the run if that meant staying together.

"You'll be okay, Ben." He pats me on the shoulder. "Believe me."

Red and blue lights are reflected on his face.

I turn around and see three squad cars outside.

"Dad! What's going on?"

I'm shaking his shoulders, but he's still just sitting there, smiling like a moron.

He looks up at me in that same sleepy slow-motion. "You'll be okay, Ben."

He stands up and walks toward the motel door.

I cry out, "Dad! Don't!"

He opens the door.

The deputies yell, "Freeze!"

Dad turns his back to the deputies, meets my eyes, "Sorry, Ben."

He then reaches into his jacket pocket and pulls out a pistol.

"What are you doing, Dad?"

He ignores me.

He turns to the doorway, to the deputies outside, then raises the pistol.

I leap toward him, desperate to halt the nightmare.

He fires the gun.

I scream.

And the deputies fire back.

I DROP to my knees as gunfire rips into the door, into the wall, and into my father.

And then nothing, but a high-pitched screaming in my ears as the world seemingly slows to a crawl all around me.

The police outside are staring into our motel room, down at my father, then up at me, their guns drawn.

I look down at my father, inches in front of me, bleeding out on the ground.

I crawl toward him.

He looks at me, with what little life he has left. His eyes are wide, scared and confused.

I want to ask why he called the cops.

Why he shot at them.

I would ask him if he's going to die, but I don't want to hear the answer, even if he knows it.

"Dad?" I say because I have no other words.

"Ben?" he says, reaching out with one shaky, bloody hand.

Our fingers touch, and then his hand falls.

His eyes are open, but there's no light inside them.

No, no, no!

I cradle him in my arms, crying, "No!!"

I can vaguely sense the police staring at us, guns still drawn. I don't know if they're coming in or saying anything. And I don't even care. Let them shoot me.

At the moment, all I want to do is hold him, as if I can somehow bring him back to life.

And then I feel a chill, so cold and deep it's as if I've plunged into arctic waters.

I'm shaking, my breath a fog coming from my mouth.

And then there's darkness. An ebony circle with spiraling azure lights followed by movement to my right.

Movement from where there should be none, where nobody could've sneaked in on me, against the wall, between the two beds and large wooden headboards.

I turn to get a better look and see nothing but a dark blur, shadows gathering into form, somehow stepping out of the wall.

The chill runs even deeper into me, and every fiber in my body tells me to get up, to run away before the shadow comes closer.

But where can I go?

I can't leave my father here, his body left to whatever this thing us.

I sit, paralyzed by fear and curiosity as the shadow takes form, into the shape of a person.

What the hell?

Its movement is fluid, far smoother and more efficient than any person I've ever seen, almost gliding instead of walking.

It stops next to us, and I stare up, trying to suss out features in the shadow creature.

It has no head, no eyes, nor mouth, but it seems to be looking at me nonetheless.

It tilts it head slightly as if regarding me.

And I can't look away.

I see a swelling of bright red light coming from my father.

I stare down, half-expecting him to be stirring back to life.

But he's not.

Instead, his body is glowing, brighter and brighter as

light gathers above him, taking a form like the shadow that
came from the wall.

I can't stop staring as my mind tries to make sense of
what I'm seeing.

The light takes the form of a person, stepping away
from us, and then it looks back at us, down to my father's
body, then at me.

Dad?

The light turns away, taking the Darkness's hand.

They walk toward the space between the beds.

"Dad!" I cry out, leaping up, trying to stop him, or
whatever is left of him, before he vanishes with the shadow.

He's already stepping into the wall.

I reach out to grab the Darkness: "No!"

As my hand touches it, time freezes again.

And I'm no longer in myself.

I'm inside of it.

I'M NO LONGER HUMAN.

I'm inside the thing that came to take my father.

I'm a shadow of a shadow.

A Collector.

One of many others.

A thing that's always been, but knows not why it is.

A thing that exists in between worlds, in The Void,
crossing into our dimension to gather passing souls and
usher them back to The Void.

It has no feelings.

It doesn't know love, nor pain, nor loss.

It has no fear.

Just an … *instinct?*

Sometimes it picks up on the feelings of a soul as it's taken. And those feelings remind it of something Before.

But it doesn't remember anything Before.

It does remember a lot about us, though.

It's collected our souls before we were anything resembling humans.

I see memories of it collecting, distant ancestors of humans, animals resembling apes. And before that, other variations of our evolutionary lifespan, going back all the way to the beginning, when we were light.

Carry the Light and deliver into The Void.

Over and over forever.

We're walking into The Void, an endless darkness.

But it's not all darkness.

There are other Collectors, shadows among shadows. But with each of them, a Light.

Are the Lights souls, like my father's, who is holding my — The Collector's — shadow hand?

There is no ground here, nor sky.

We're all walking, or floating, in the abyss, floating in a spiral pattern. In the center of that spiral is a bright white light.

As I look at it, I feel something swelling inside me, even though there is no *me* here.

A loud shriek and chattering respond to my awe — as if it's suddenly aware of me in its body.

It isn't happy that I'm here.

Or maybe it's warning me.

The chattering gets louder.

Then it spreads to all of The Collectors.

The spiral formation stops.

And all at once I feel a million, maybe more, stares in my direction.

The Light in the center of everything explodes without a sound.

~

AND JUST LIKE THAT, I'm back in my body, back in the shitty motel, back holding my father's lifeless body.

Back with the police guns trained on me.

And I've never felt more alone.

Chapter Eight

Ben Shepherd Age 17

~

11 Days later

~

I'M SITTING in the pew with Aunt Trudy by my side, holding her hand, waiting for my father's funeral service to start. I'm supposed to be crying, but I've already emptied my eyes in the past week. I doubt I have a single tear left.

Not sure I have *anything* left.

I feel numb.

Ever since the motel room shootout, and The Collectors, I feel like I've been living in a nightmare. The church is nearly empty, at least of people I know. Reporters outside want to ask the questions I've been asking myself.

Why did he snap?

Why did he shoot at the deputies?

71

Was he trying commit suicide by cop?

Nothing else made any sense. Why else open fire? If he truly wanted to kill them, he wouldn't have missed every shot.

So what *did* happen?

I've seen "experts" on TV suggest everything from drugs to medication to a contempt for authority — even though there's no evidence for that last one. If he were a terrorist or psycho with a grudge, he would've had a manifesto or something.

Aunt Trudy is beside herself with grief. She's tried talking to me, telling me "I'm here for you" and other things to make me feel better, but she's just as confused.

She asked me if Dad said anything to me. I told her all I knew — that he'd seemed on edge and I think it had something to do with work. I didn't mention the argument with Willow's father, as I don't think it's why he snapped, and I don't want her forbidding me from seeing my girlfriend.

Willow has called a few times, but I haven't seen her since my Dad picked me up so we could run off to Mexico.

Mostly, I've been busy with Trudy, talking to police and black-suited men. They didn't say who they worked for, but I'm guessing it's Dad.

The police — and the men in black — turned our house inside out and upside down. I'm not sure what they were searching for, or if they found anything. Maybe they were looking for some evidence that would explain what the hell made my dad snap.

Or cover it up.

I try not to let paranoid thoughts take root. I don't want to follow in my father's footsteps. But I can't help but think that maybe something was going on. Maybe he discovered something he wasn't supposed to, and running was all he could do.

I keep looking behind me, wondering if Willow will show. None of my other friends have. Not that I had that many.

Apparently, neither did my father.

I look around the room. There's a handful of strangers and a few people who live on our street. A few came up to Trudy and me, offering words that were supposed to make us feel better, but all of the *I'm sorry* in the world won't bring my father back.

Sorry.

Such a horrible word to offer someone in mourning. You'd think after all these years adults would have finally found something more appropriate, something better than *sorry*.

Sorry is what you say when you spill milk, not when someone dies.

If Willow *does* show, she better not say "sorry" or I'll probably scream.

The preacher steps up to the lectern in front of my father's closed casket. He looks at me, then around the room.

He starts to speak, more words intended to comfort the living. At least he's not saying "sorry."

The doors open in the rear. Then Willow enters with her parents. My eyes well up as if I've been waiting for her presence to help me cry.

Don't be a pussy. Man up, Ben!

They make their way around the pews, heading toward us.

I stand to greet Willow.

She hugs me. Tight.

At least she doesn't say sorry.

Mr. Fairchild and his wife shake hands with Trudy and me.

His wife says, "I'm sorry for your loss."

They sit.

Willow's hand finds its way into mine as the preacher talks about a bunch of stuff my father didn't believe in. I wonder if he thinks my dad is in Heaven.

I wonder if my father's in Heaven.

If there even is *a Heaven.*

Is heaven a Void?

Collectors lined up waiting to toss your soul into a white hole?

The priest finishes his bit, then asks if anyone would like to say something.

Trudy unfolds a crumpled piece of paper she'd been clutching since we sat. Stuff she spent all morning on. I wrote something, too, but I'm not sure if I'll be able to read my words without breaking down.

Trudy approaches the lectern and starts telling a story about how her older brother was always there for her. How when they were little kids, he always let her play with him, stuck up for her, and even beat up some boy who made her cry.

She gets a few laughs, then breaks down crying.

And now I'm crying too.

Willow's fingers squeeze tight around mine.

Trudy slowly regains her composure.

She can't finish.

She leaves the lectern.

The preacher asks if anyone else wants to say anything.

I do, but I can't.

I'm crying too hard, and if I go up there, I doubt I'll be able to get a single word out.

I continue looking at the ground, feeling awful that the

words I'd written for this service, in honor of my father, will never be uttered.

WE'RE STANDING in the hall outside the church, people I don't know talking about my father, telling stories about how nice he was to them. But none of them were truly his friends, and they're telling the lamest stories ever, like how he once changed this old lady's tire or how he once bought ten boxes of Girl Scout cookies to help this man's daughter win some prize.

Jesus, this is sad.

I'm desperate to get out.

Trudy is trapped talking with a few neighbors.

Thankfully, I have Willow as a buffer. As long as I stand here talking to her, most people will leave me alone. Her parents are with Trudy, trapped, too, talking to complete strangers.

Willow grabs my arm, "come on."

She brings me through a door into the rear of the church, and out the back doors.

Outside, she pulls a joint from her purse and lights it.

I'm surprised, as I've never seen her smoke anything, let alone pot. But then again, even after all this time she's still sometimes a mystery.

She smiles at my surprise. "You never smoked?"

"Um, no!" I say, as if she just asked if I ever shot up a train station.

She laughs. "You need to relax."

She takes a deep drag, then passes it to me.

I hold the joint gingerly in my fingers, unsure of what to do, feeling stupid.

"Inhale and hold it."

I do.

Fire fills my chest, and I cough, unable to hold anything.

She laughs, taking it back, then demonstrates the proper way again.

"Aren't you afraid people will smell this on us?"

"Your dad just died. They'll get over it."

She hands me the joint.

I inhale again, holding it, barely suppressing a cough.

"Now breathe it out," she says.

As I do, she comes in and kisses me.

It's not a sensual kiss, so much as a comforting one. "This sucks."

We hug.

I thank her for not saying "sorry."

We finish the joint, and I feel a bit lighter, a bit calmer. I'm wondering if I'm supposed to feel giggly or hungry or something, but at the moment, I'm not feeling much of either.

She sprays us both with perfume.

"Would you rather smell like Cheech n' Chong?" she asks.

"Like *who?*"

She laughs.

I'm not sure why, but her laughter invites some of my own.

We make our way back to the others, and now I'm afraid I'll start laughing at my dad's funeral service. That would be awful.

And the more I think about it, the funnier it seems.

I make my way to the restroom, then burst out laughing.

It doesn't take long before the giggly mood is replaced by a crushing depression as I think about Willow and what will happen next. There's no way I can afford the Academy now. I'll probably have to go back to a public school where I don't know anyone and won't fit in for anything.

All traces of humor gone, I leave the bathroom and find Willow's father standing with Aunt Trudy.

She waves me over.

I hope they can't smell the weed beneath the perfume.

Trudy says, "Mr. Fairchild just gave us some great news."

I look for Willow. She's with her mom, talking to some other people. I wonder if she already knows the nature of this news.

I look at Mr. Fairchild and try to offer my best smile. "What's that?"

"The Headmaster and I agree that it would be a shame for you to leave the Academy. We're going to waive your tuition and dorm costs through graduation. And after you graduate, you can get a job at AD while taking university courses online."

"What?" I can hardly believe it. "I can stay?"

"Yes. If you want to."

Trudy is smiling. It's hard to read her expression since she's so good at faking it, but I *think* she's cool with this.

"Yeah, I want to! Thank you, Mr. Fairchild," I say, shaking his hand.

He pulls me into a hug. "You're welcome, son."

Chapter Nine

Ben Shepherd Age 19

I'M SITTING ALONE in one of the many labs at AD eating a turkey and Swiss on rye that Willow packed in my lunch last night, waiting for Kotke to show so we can run the latest numbers.

Willow and I got a place together, and both took jobs here after graduating the Academy, though she finished a year before me. To call it a "job" is a bit of a stretch. I'm basically doing the same things I was doing at school, helping to evolve a few Top Secret projects which will hopefully someday prepare us to save Willow. But now I'm being paid.

My powers, as Kotke calls them, are growing more by the day, though it's hard to measure the progress when there's so much I don't know about the project I'm working on.

Everything at AD is part of a "project." Most have a

Top Secret classification, requiring a ton of signed paper-work before I can even start. My current projects are Project Snowblind and Project Lantern. I only know about the things I'm involved in, and am given no line of sight to each project's primary purpose.

I work on two different things at AD, improving my telepathic communication with humans (Project Snow-blind), and telepathically communicating with electronics and computers (Project Lantern).

I'm told that both will prepare me for my role in Project Willow, which I assume is a project to save her, though I, nor Willow, have any clue how. And I hate that they have me doing all of this computer work. I don't see how that's anywhere near as important as the mind stuff. Even as hard as that is on me, body and soul, the work is rewarding. Every time I ask why, I'm told that I need a full understanding. Eventually I'm supposed to be able to transfer information from a computer network to a human soul. That sounds impossible to me.

Willow's been working on another project with her father, though she's not allowed to tell me what it was. I assume it has something to do with her psychic powers, but who knows, maybe she's counting mustard packets from some Top Secret Mustard Spy thing.

Even after more than a year here, I still haven't learned what my father did for AD. Given the size of the place, and the number of employees, he could've been anything from civilian to spy. I asked Mr. Fairchild once, but he said that Dad was "a consultant."

I've thought about trying to probe his mind, but I'm not particularly good at it, even with test subjects willing to let me, let alone someone who guards against it. Though Willow hasn't confirmed it, I fully suspect that her father is a Deviant, too. And I'm guessing that his power is telepathic in some way.

As I'm about to ball up my paper lunch bag, I feel something hard at the bottom of the bag.

Under the folded paper towels at the bottom, I find a red cardboard heart.

I pull it out, smiling as I see Willow's handwriting on the front:

I LOVE YOU

I turn it over and see more words on the back:

SEE YOU TONIGHT

XXX

Tonight is one of the nights she's supposed to be most fertile.

We've been trying for six months. Ideally, we would've waited until we were more established or at least in our twenties, but Willow's convinced that she doesn't have much time and wants to enjoy a few years of motherhood before she dies.

We used to argue about it a lot.

I asked, why bring a child into the world if you think you're going to die? Why do that to a baby?

She argued that the whole point of life is to create more life. And she wanted to leave her mark on this world in some way or another, so some part of her lives on.

And who the hell am I to say that's a bad reason to have a baby?

I might have argued more if we were poor young kids struggling to get by. But between her father's wealth and the surprise insurance money I got a year after my father's death, our child will be fine.

Oddly, even though she wants to start a family, Willow doesn't want to get married. She says that there's no point in making it more difficult for me when I want to settle down with someone else down the road. And since we don't have a child, we're not *really* a family. There's something sad about that sentiment. Made sadder by the fact that we haven't been able to conceive.

I wonder if I'm sterile. And if so, should we look into some other method of getting her pregnant? I hate being the thing keeping Willow from having a family of her own.

I wipe a tear from my eye as I place the heart in my front shirt pocket, then crumple the bag and toss it to the garbage can across the room.

The shot bounces off the rim of and hits the shiny white tiled floor.

I stand to pick it up.

The door behind me opens.

Kotke.

"Sorry I'm late, Ben. Got stuck in traffic on my lunch break."

He isn't alone. Arnold Fairchild is behind him, impeccably dressed as usual in his white suit and red rose.

"Ben," he says, shaking my hand firmly. "Good to see you."

When we meet on the occasional weekend dinner at his house, he gives me a bear hug. But on the rare times when he comes to the research labs, it's always a firm handshake.

"Good to see you too, sir," I say, surprised that he's here.

"Mr. Kotke shared the latest numbers," he says, cutting right to the chase.

"And?"

"You've come a long way. We think you're ready."

"Ready for what?" I ask, looking and back and forth between the men.

"Ready to start on Project Eden."

∼

AFTER A LONG WALK down several hallways and a trip down multiple floors in an elevator I didn't know existed, I'm standing with Kotke and Fairchild in a short hallway outside a pair of double doors.

An armed guard nods us through.

I follow the men into a long, dark, cold rectangular room with nothing inside it. Despite the emptiness, there's a low humming and a constant rush of cold air coming through the vents above.

The men stop in the middle of the room. Just as I'm wondering if this is a hazing ritual, Kotke bends down and pulls at an inconspicuous handle set into the floor.

This triggers a sound like something unlocking and a long hiss of air.

He backs up as large glass tube rises from the ground.

I fall back, startled.

The tube extends all the way to the ceiling, then stops, followed by a rattle of locks turning beneath it.

The hiss fades.

Red lights inside the tube snap on, illuminating the girl inside.

"Ben," Mr. Fairchild says, "meet Eden."

Chapter Ten

Ben Shepherd Age 19

"WHO IS SHE?" I stare into the tube, at a girl who can't be more than seven.

She has long red hair and is wearing a white jumper like most of our test subjects. She looks a lot like Willow in pictures from when she was younger.

Her eyes are closed.

Is she sleeping?

Is she dead?

"This is Eden. Willow's twin sister."

"Sister?"

"They were seven-years-old when Eden died. Willow doesn't like to talk about her. Plus, Eden is *very* top secret."

"She's a Deviant?" I ask.

"Yes," Fairchild says.

"What was her power?"

"She was a Jumper," Fairchild says. "Mr. Kotke, can you please explain to Ben what a Jumper is."

Kotke tells me about Deviants who can Jump into the bodies of other people. There aren't many, and most can't control it. It isn't uncommon for Jumpers to lose their minds and commit suicide. He explains his theory of self as soul, and that it's the Jumpers' souls making the trips into other bodies.

Fairchild stands there as Kotke talks, staring at the girl in the tube. I can practically taste his sadness. And there's another emotion. One that surprises me: *hope*. And with that hope, fear.

"Is that what happened to her?" I ask.

"No," Kotke shakes his head. "We were monitoring her body after a Jump when something went wrong with her vitals. Specifically, she went into cardiac arrest and died. We couldn't revive her."

"Shit. So what happened to her soul?"

Kotke sighs. "We don't know for certain."

"Bullshit," Fairchild says, turning around. "She's lost in The Void."

The sound of that word — *the memory* — stops my heart.

I approach the tube, staring at the girl.

She doesn't look dead. She looks asleep.

"Is she in a coma?"

Fairchild looks back at me, shaking his head. "No. Her body is dead. We've preserved her using state-of-the-art technology decades ahead of anything else."

"Why?"

Fairchild's eyes widen, and his brows go up as if I slapped him across the face.

Shit! I think I've offended him.

"Why? Because you are going to transfer Willow's soul

into Eden's body."

"What?"

Kotke steps toward me. "*This* is what we've been working toward. And the first phase starts now. We've installed a fully-functioning AI into Eden's body. We need you to make the connection. Turn the engines on, so to speak."

An AI? An actual artificial intelligence? I wasn't aware that AD was working on AI, but I guess I shouldn't be surprised. They have their fingers in deviant education, biotech, psychic warfare, pharmaceuticals, and who knows what else?

"How the hell am I going to turn Eden on?"

"Don't worry, son," Fairchild slaps my back, "You'll figure it out."

I'M STANDING in front of the examination table where Eden lies motionless.

We're alone in the lab, but I can still feel eyes on me from behind the overhead two-way mirrors.

They're all counting on me to do something that I've never done. Something that *nobody* has ever done.

They want me to wake the dead.

But is it waking the dead if Eden's soul isn't there? According to Fairchild, her soul isn't. I don't know how he can tell. Maybe his telepathic abilities allow him to see inside her.

I'm supposed to connect to her like the others, like the computers I send and receive data from telepathically. But she isn't like the others, awake and functioning. Even if they put chips in her brain, she isn't a computer. She's more of a cyborg — if I can wake her/it up.

I close my eyes and focus on her.

I can usually sense an opening. In computers and people, there are often ways in. It's like a doorway. My mind knocks, and I enter.

I don't know *how* I do it. I don't know how I do much of what I do. While I've managed to gain some control over my powers, I have no knowledge of the *hows* or *whys*. And theories aren't answers.

In training, Kotke tells me not to think about the hows and whys, to focus on what feels right. He compares most Deviants' powers to the instinctual things that humans simply know how to do. We don't learn to breathe, blink, open our eyes, or suck from the tit. These actions exist in a biological knowledge base passed down from our ancestors' ancestors. Same with Deviant powers.

I keep searching for the opening but sense nothing in the girl. I can barely feel a body in the room with me, or any electronics, save those in the walls and in the rooms around me.

If she has a way in, it's a signal lost in the noise.

I think about this project and what it means for Willow. I wonder if she knows that her twin's body is in a container, preserved as a child. I wonder if she knows that her father intends to transfer her soul into her sister's body.

Are we even close to doing this?

We can't possibly transfer a soul from one body to another. How does one even find a soul? Science, as far as I know, still debates the *existence* of a soul. But Fairchild and crew say there is one, and that Eden's soul jumped from body to body and was eventually lost to The Void.

He called her a Jumper and said there were others. How many? And how do they jump?

Can Willow Jump too? Is it something she'll need to learn before she can Jump into Eden's body? Or am I somehow involved? They said I would be transferring her soul. But *how?* What does that mean? A soul isn't a packet of data you can transfer from one body to another.

Or is it?

My mind fills with the noise I've learned to silence — the static, the electronic transmissions, the electric hum, exploding suns from millions of light years away.

As a child, I didn't understand the sounds, and they overwhelmed me. Kotke helped me gain control, learn to tune it out, then eventually to receive and decipher transmissions.

I listen for Eden.

How I can recognize a particular person's sound is another thing I don't understand. And my track record is far from perfect.

As I push all the other sounds from my mind, I finally hear it, like a fluctuating musical note rising and lowering ever so slightly.

First I hear it, then I see it in my mind — a light pink aura radiating from Eden's body.

Weird how I hadn't sensed it before, but now that I've stripped away the other sounds, it's as obvious as neon at nighttime.

I focus, changing my signal to match hers.

And then I'm inside.

I'm usually aware of my body when I go inside someone's mind. It's like I'm virtually touring their memories — a mess of tangled thoughts, scents, sounds, and tastes.

I struggle, sorting through memories until I find something I can work with, something close to *complete*, though memories aren't finished objects like a video tape, but bits and pieces that are far more likely to be recalled out of sequence than in anything resembling an experiential memory.

But here there is only the hum.

No visuals.

No thoughts.

No sights.

No tastes.

It feels empty and cold.

And I can't feel my body.

Is this what the Jumpers feel like when they wind up in someone else?

Have I jumped?

I can't panic.

Have to focus.

The biological hardwiring that sits inside every human has a gossamer bond to the chips. I need to seep inside those seams.

I focus on the mechanical hum and radiate a similar energy pattern, pouring myself into it.

There's a blinding flash of light and sound so loud and so intense that I'm kicked out of her body, and thrown back into mine.

The pain is instant. Intense. A fire is consuming my body.

I scream as I slam into the wall behind me, then slump to the ground.

I feel like I touched a live wire and got knocked on my ass.

The pain is over as quickly as it came, but it's hard to focus or find my bearings.

I finally manage to sit up and open my eyes.

Movement pulls my gaze to the table.

I look up and see Eden sitting up.

I stare, my heart racing, as she opens her eyes and looks right at me.

"Hello, Ben," she says.

Chapter Eleven

Ben Shepherd Age 19

≈

LATER THAT DAY …

≈

WILLOW and I are waiting in an overstuffed leather love seat in Mr. Fairchild's private library at AD, where he holds most of his private meetings.

Willow knows that he has big news — good news — but she doesn't know what and I've been sworn to secrecy.

She's sitting on the couch beside me, anxiously bouncing one leg over the other, biting her nails.

"You sure you haven't had any visions?" I ask, "Because this is a pretty big deal."

"Stop teasing me!"

I laugh, but that can't hide the anxiety I'm feeling for Willow. I don't think she has any clue that her father has preserved Eden's body. That's Potential Freakout Number One.

When she learns that he's put a computer into her sister? Well, that's Potential Freakout Number Two.

And that he plans to put her soul into her sister's body when she dies?

Yeah, that's a Freakout Hat-Trick.

Willow crosses her arms. "I can't believe that you know and Dad won't tell me."

I desperately want to tell her, but I can't. "Jealous?" I say, like a coward.

She gives me a cross look.

She looks adorable when pouty, but I'm not about to tell her that.

At times like this I usually giggle, but right now I can't. Not when I'm so unsure of how this whole thing is going to go down. And if she's mad at her father, will she be mad that I didn't warn her?

Of course she will be. And she would have every right.

This is an ambush and Willow has no idea. She says she's never read my mind and I believe her. She's one of the most scrupulous people I've ever met. Just another one of the many reasons that I love her so much.

She has to know.

"Willow, there's something you need to—"

The door opens, and Mr. Fairchild enters the room.

He's alone. For now.

He closes the door, hugs his daughter, then sits on one of the two chairs across from us.

He folds his hands over his lap and begins a preamble to prepare her.

"Please, Dad," Willow interrupts. "Cut to the chase."

He sighs, then takes out his phone and makes a call. "Yes, come in."

Moments later, Kotke enters with Eden, wearing a blue dress and white patent leather shoes.

Then Kotke leaves the room and closes the door behind him.

Willow gasps as she stands.

"Eden?" She steps closer, her eyes wide. "How?"

"Hello, Willow. I'm sorry to disappoint you, but I'm not your sister. This *is* her body, perfectly preserved since her soul's departure. I am an Artificial Intelligence. You may call me Eden."

Tears well up in Willow's eyes.

Her face is turning red as she steps closer, reaches out, touches the girl's skin. Then she spins around and screams, "What did you do?"

Fairchild raises his hands, open-palmed, "I did this for you, Willow. Eden's body will be a vessel for your soul once you pass."

She turns back to the girl, then to her father, her face redder, her mouth twisted in agony as she shakes her head.

"You ... you never told me you kept Eden's body alive."

"She's not alive. She was preserved. For *you*. I promised that we would find a way for you to live on. And now we have. Ben can transfer your soul into her. We're going to map your mind so we can upload a copy of your physical mind along with your soul. You won't be a copy or a clone. You will be you."

"You never said you were going to use Eden's body!"

Willow's shoulders slump. She closes her eyes, balling her fists.

I've never seen her so angry.

My gut and my heart ache for her.

I want to get her away.

I want to apologize for not telling her.

I want to make this all go away.

I want to hug her, to try to do something to show some support, but I'm getting a strong feeling of anger towards me, too.

If I touch her now, she might tear my head off.

Eden reaches out and touches her shoulder. "I'm sorry, Willow."

She flinches. Recoils. "Don't touch me!"

Then she turns her angry gaze on me. "You knew about this?"

"I only learned today, Willow. But—"

"No buts," she says, throwing up a finger to silence me.

She spins back to her father, "I don't want any part of this!"

Willow gives Eden an extra-wide berth as she storms out of the library and slams the door.

I look at Eden, expecting to see the girl on the verge of tears. Instead, she stares straight ahead, awaiting input or stimuli.

Like a fucking robot.

I stare at the door, then turn to a glowering Mr. Fairchild.

"You need to fix this, Ben," he says.

Chapter Twelve

Ben Shepherd Age 20

~

WE'RE EATING at Cafe Beaujolais for Willow's twenty-first birthday.

We're sitting in the back, where it's dark, quiet, and romantic. I had wanted to throw a surprise party, but Willow talked me out of it, particularly since her father already threw her one last weekend at his house.

At least they're finally getting along again.

It took a few months for her to get used to his plan, even if she's yet to spend much real time with Eden or do any of the mapping of her brain that we need to do if we're going at this from both a brain and soul approach.

We don't have much time left, and nobody's sure how long the mind mapping will take. I feel like we should've started five years ago.

I wonder how many years we really have left.

I figure at least four, assuming her prophecy is correct.

But what if she's sick for a long time and only has a year or two of a quality life left?

We finish dinner, and the waiter appears, as planned, with the cake I'd brought over earlier, lit with twenty-one pink and red candles.

Willow glares at me with that fake angry look that she gives me when I pull something like this.

Several other servers appear to sing *Happy Birthday*.

"Thank you," she says.

The waiter cuts and plates two pieces of cake then wishes Willow one last happy birthday before leaving us alone.

"When did you do this?"

I smile. "On my lunch break."

"I wondered why you were working through your lunch break. And here I was pissed that you weren't taking me to lunch on my birthday!"

I smile wider, then press my fork into the cake — decadent chocolate with vanilla frosting from Vanessa's Baking Company. Her favorite.

My fork hits something.

What the—?

Something shiny is inside my cake.

I reach in, and my finger slides through a metal hole.

Did someone lose a ring in this cake?

I pull it out. It's a men's wedding band.

"Ew, I think the baker dropped a ring in the cake," I say, unsure if I want to eat any of it.

Willow laughs.

"Or, maybe someone at this table outsmarted her boyfriend. Maybe this certain fiery redhead knew he would get a cake from Vanessa's, then called Vanessa ahead of time and told her to put a ring in the cake, and told the waiter to cut the piece with the "H" on it and give it to you."

"But why?"

She laughs. "Wow, for a smart guy, you are *damned* clueless."

And then it hits me.

"Oh, my God. Are you saying you want to marry me?"

I'm tearing up. And thanks to the proposal, I was already feeling too much like a girl.

"Yes." She gets down on one knee and holds out her hand, asking for the ring.

I wipe off the pieces of cake and place it in her palm.

She's about to slide it on my finger and reverse tradition, but then she stops.

"Oh, wait, I almost forgot," she says, reaching over to her purse, pulling something out, palming it, then sliding it into my hand.

"First this."

I look down.

It's a pregnancy test. With two lines.

"Does this say what I think it does?" I ask, tears now flowing.

She's crying too, smiling as she nods.

I hug her. "Yes!"

Diners applaud all around us, but there's no way they can possibly know how happy I am.

Chapter Thirteen

Ben Shepherd Age 21

～

"I CAN'T DO IT," Willow cries, still pushing.

Her face is red. Sweat beads her brow. The light above her bed feels like a heat lamp.

She's been in labor for nearly twelve hours. She's exhausted, barely able to push.

I sit beside her bed in a chair, doing my best to be there for support without annoying her. She's normally laid back and good-natured, quick with humor, but now she feels only pain and exhaustion. She's already yelled at her parents to wait outside because her mom kept trying to "help out."

Willow refused a C-section, but by the thirteenth hour, I wonder if she's regretting her decision. I try to encourage her.

"You can do it! You've *got this*, honey."

I give her my hand for support.

She grips it tight enough to turn my fingers all white.

I don't pull away. If she needs to break every one of my fingers to get through childbirth, then so be it.

Willow's doctor coaches her. "That's it, Willow. Push."

She screams, squeezing my hand even tighter.

"You've got it, baby. You've got it."

She continues to push, her entire body now trembling.

I focus on her face. I can't stand the thought of looking anywhere else.

"I can't do it!" Willow screams, collapsing, her hand relenting its iron grip on my fingers.

I move closer, hoping my presence doesn't annoy her.

Willow looks up at me, a wreck.

And here I sit, helpless to make this any better.

She's the only one who can do this.

I lean over, kiss her on the forehead, and whisper, "You've got this, baby."

She begins to push again, gritting her teeth against the pain.

Suddenly, a cry.

I turn to see the doctor pulling a baby from between my wife's legs.

Willow is looking up, tears streaming down her cheeks, smiling as she stares.

Then the doctor hands our daughter to Willow, umbilical cord still attached.

She takes the tiny pink baby against her bosom, nuzzling her cheek against its little, fuzzy head.

Willow looks up at me, and for the first time, I understand what she meant: Having a baby completes our family.

And I will do *anything* to keep our family together.

Chapter Fourteen

Ben Shepherd Age 22

I STARE at the old man in the examination bed wondering if he ever thought he'd be part of medical history.

We're in an operating theater in the bowels of AD.

The man is hooked up to machines monitoring his heart rate and blood pressure.

Thank God he's asleep. I'm not sure I could do this with him awake, even if he consented in exchange for whatever ungodly sum of money Advanced Dynamic paid his family.

His name is Oliver Remington, an 87-year-old plumber who had what little life he had left cut short by an aggressive brain tumor.

He went downhill fast. One week he was vital, walking around, and the next, he was having memory problems, complaining of pain.

Then he turned angry and scared.

One of his doctors reached out to AD, who'd asked key people to keep an eye out for potential subjects for Project Willow.

Kotke is beside me, and there are three doctors with us.

Fairchild is on the other side of the two-way mirrors above us, probably with other members of Advanced Dynamics, sitting and watching, waiting for us all to make history.

One of the doctors, a thin, older black man with intense eyes whom I've never met, says, "Are you ready?"

I nod, even though I'm terrified that this isn't going to work.

Terrified that we're about to kill a man for nothing.

Yes, he was going to die anyway, and at least this way he'll go out painlessly, with his family well-compensated after his passing, but still, we're killing a man for something that might not fly.

I shake the doubt from my head.

I remember *why* I'm doing this.

Willow's been withdrawn in recent weeks. Her depression is always worst in the aftermath of her mind mapping sessions with Eden.

She's not sick yet, but damn if she doesn't seem like she's preparing for death. Sometimes I wonder if she knows something she's not telling me. If she does know the exact date. And if so, why not tell her father or me so we can accelerate the process?

Her only happy times are spent with Ella, who is now starting to walk. They play in our yard, following our move into the Fairchild's guest house. They go to the park. They watch shows together. Ella tries to exercise with Willow.

I wonder if Willow misses her job, or having something to do beyond staying home with Ella all day. Given how she gets cold towards me so often when I talk about work,

I have to wonder if she's jealous that I'm there and she's not.

It's not like she can't go back.

She *wanted* to stay home.

She *wants* to spend every possible second being a mother.

So why does she seem to resent me?

Doesn't she see that the long hours I put in with her father are all designed to save her life, or at least allow her to live on in another body?

I think that's part of it.

She's still not pleased that her father kept Eden alive.

She insists that it's wrong the few times we've discussed it. And creepy. She doesn't want to be in a child's body. She wants to be an adult.

Nobody seems to be sure if Eden will grow now that she's "alive," or if putting her body "on pause" for so long did something to prevent her from aging permanently.

"Here we go," Kotke says, watching the doctor inject his patient.

In a few minutes, the man's organs will shut down.

I have to capture his soul before it leaves his body, then transfer that soul into Eden. In theory, it should work, even if I understand so little about *how*.

I focus until I find his signal.

I grab his hand, and instantly we're connected.

I find myself, or the astral projection of myself, standing on a giant, dark stage without any floor or walls or ceiling or lights.

Memories rush by on fast-moving shivering walls. They're ephemeral if I watch them, but when they brush into me, the dark stage vanishes, and I'm suddenly transported into this man's memories.

They find me like bullets, piercing me, one after another.

I'm seeing through his eyes at different points in his life. Oliver as a child, playing with his brother; the time he accidentally ran over his family's dog and had to lie to his children so they wouldn't hate him; the time he asked his wife to marry him. Those memories, and thousands of others.

So far I've only done practice runs of this with two other patients.

I followed the soul's signal in both patients, which I could sense by its tone, compared to the rest of the body's noise.

I had to follow the sound and enter the person's memory.

Then I tune everything out: the memories, the chatter, everything.

I listen for his soul.

I hear it, up and to my right, inside a wall of memory.

I push myself toward it like a swimmer underwater.

I splash into the wall and find myself on a porch on a hot summer day in Kansas when Oliver was nine.

He's sitting on the porch swing of his parent's old run-down farmhouse, petting his puppy — a beagle named Sparky.

He smiles at his puppy.

His family struggled to put food on the table, but life was simple.

And there, just behind him, I see what I've come to find.

His soul.

It's an energy that science and all its machines cannot sense.

But my gifts display it with clarity.

I see the aura more than the soul, and in Oliver's case,

his is bright blue, surrounding a fist-sized orb floating behind him.

Inside the aura, that clear nothingness, is his soul.

Despite having seen several, nobody has told me how to take it.

Fairchild said to trust my instincts.

That means *I have no fucking idea, son.*

With computers and memories, I've so far been able to visualize and grab, bringing them back with me or placing them into others, my interface manufactured on the fly.

But behind the scenes is work that I can't understand.

I reach out with my disembodied hand and touch it, unsure of what will happen. But my fingers feel nothing

They pass through the soul. It simply slips away.

His aura blinks red before it vanishes, kicking me out of the memory and back into the black stage of his mind.

Shit!

Beeps in the real world signal that Oliver is about to die.

Again I search for the signal, but the walls of memory are racing by at the speed of light, spinning into a blinding white cacophony.

I try to focus on the tone, but can't hear it beneath the screaming river of memories crashing over and into me.

One second I'm standing on a Miami street corner at midnight, the next I'm in bed with his wife.

Then I'm an infant crawling on the floor.

His life is racing by as his body shuts down.

I have to find his soul then figure out how to capture it!

If not, this whole thing is a failure.

How do I find something the size of a fist in all of this?

Beyond his memories, I feel emotions, everything he's ever felt in his life: joy, fear, hate, lust, heartbreak, envy … so much sadness.

If his life was a song, it's defining note would be sorrow.

So much heartache.

Hopelessness begins to drown me.

Memories darken in tenor and visibility.

I *must* find his soul.

Then I remember one of the first memories, the one where he accidentally ran over his dog.

I propel myself through the walls of memory hoping that whatever guides my powers — instinct or supernatural force — will lead me true.

And then I'm there, standing on his front lawn watching his car backing up. He is going to pick up his children from elementary school and unaware that the family dog — a big, lovable mutt named Clyde — had gotten out of the house and is lying on the driveway, baking in the sun.

THUMP!

And a yelp.

Oliver stops and leaps out of his car.

"Oh God," he cries out, staring down at Clyde's body beneath the Toyota. The dog is looking up at him, confused, its eyes glassy as blood spills from beneath him.

"No, no, no, no. Clyde, I'm so sorry."

He drops to his knees, trying to pull the dog out from under the car, but realizes that it's stuck. Even if it weren't, nothing could save him now.

He cries.

Behind him, I see his soul, floating, surrounded by a dark black aura, pulsating, growing while the memory darkens at the edges.

Oliver's body is shutting down.

Soon, there will be nothing.

And still, I don't know what to do. How to capture Oliver's soul.

An idea finds me.

Until now, I've been an unseen spectator in this man's mind, but I can make myself visible. So I do.

I approach Oliver. He looks up at me, confused, scared, crying.

"My dog. I killed my dog."

His soul hovers behind him, pulsating, growing darker, the aura blooming larger as the clear part shrinks, as if the aura would soon consume the soul.

"I can help you," I say.

"How?"

"I can make this go away."

He looks at me confused. "What do you mean *go away?*"

"I can take this pain away. I can bring your dog back," I lie, desperate for his trust.

"How?"

"You need to take my hand."

He looks at it uncertainly, suddenly a child, looking up at me, scared and crying. "Take your hand, and it goes away?"

"Yes," I say, trusting an idea that's really only a hope.

He reaches out and takes my hand.

And then it happens.

His soul crashes into him.

His hand locks onto mine.

And then the pain, *his pain*, is coursing through me, starting at my hands and winding its way through my body.

But not just his pain, but every other emotion, spreading through me like a white-hot fire licking log cabin walls.

Then it's all I can feel.

My instinct wants to let go, but I can't.

This is how I take his soul.

And then, darkness.

I open my eyes.

I'm back in the operating theater.

The beeping machine swears that Oliver's dead.

I'm overwhelmed by sorrow as I stare at my body.

No, not mine. Oliver's.

And then confusion as his memories tangle with my own.

I turn to Kotke to tell him I don't feel well.

Then I crash to the ground.

I WAKE TO A BLUR.

I'm sitting at the circular table in Eden's room. Not the room she lives in, but the one where she talks with me and Willow, where we've done most of our experiments.

Kotke is next to me and Eden is across the table.

"What happened?" I ask.

More of Oliver's memories rip through me.

I'm standing in his driveway again, but now it's me getting out of the car and looking down at my dead dog.

What the hell?

"Can you hear me?" Kotke's voice pulls me back into the real world. "What's happening?"

"His memories … they're too much."

"I was afraid of this. I think his soul is trying to take control of you."

"What?"

How can he even know this?

Did he work with the Jumper program too?

Is this a common thing?

Kotke grabs my hand. "You need to get it out of you. Focus on uploading it to Eden."

Eden looks at me with that weird artificial smile that creeps Willow out as much as it does me. In her little girl's voice, she says, "Are you ready, Ben?"

"Yes," I say, forging the connection with her as I have hundreds of times before while she's mapped my mind to learn and perfect the Project.

As we connect, I find myself in another of Oliver's memories, this time I'm running through a burning house searching for my daughter.

No, not mine, *his*.

I have to find her!

"Focus," Kotke says, grabbing my hand tight, pulling me back.

And then I connect with Eden.

Her inner space is unlike the darkness of most people's. Whenever I enter her mind, we're in Fairchild's enormous estate, usually in her bedroom. I'm not sure if this is a residual memory that Eden had of the house — I'm told there shouldn't be any — or a computer simulation designed to create a stable space for our interaction.

She appears in the space looking the same as she does in life, like a child.

"Hello, Ben. What have you brought me?"

I look behind me and see the soul is no longer a small fist-sized ball, but rather an unwieldy mess of darkness. A scribble come to life.

Shaped like a human.

Did I change its shape, or is this what happens to the soul once it's in a new host?

"Take its hand," I say.

She reaches out and takes it.

The scribble-mess vanishes.

And then I'm out of her mind.

I exhale, relieved not to feel the pain of Oliver's soul trying to assert control over me. Then I look at Eden, whose face has changed.

She's no longer wearing her usual, vacant expression.

Now she looks confused.

"Who are you people?" she asks, looking from me to Kotke.

"Who are you?" Kotke asks.

"Oliver. Oliver Remington."

Kotke smiles. "Oh my God, I think it worked."

Chapter Fifteen

Ben Shepherd Age 23

I'M in the drive-through lane at Dunkin Donuts picking up a dozen donuts, coffee, and hot cocoa to surprise Willow and Ella before they wake up.

It's cold in the car, the streets are slick with snow, and I'm stuffed up, coming down with something that's completely blocked my sense of smell. I'm anxious for the cocoa to kill some of the stuffiness.

It's been three months since our breakthrough. Surprisingly, Eden can control Oliver's soul, allowing our access whenever we want.

Despite the success, I can't help but feel cruel when speaking to Oliver through Eden. He's confused, asking why he's stuck in this body, why can't he leave the facility, and why I didn't help him like I promised.

I've asked Kotke and Mr. Fairchild when we can let the man go, as they've assured me that his soul can be released.

But neither are prepared to do so just yet. They want to keep him for long term study, not just to determine the feasibility of using Eden's body for Willow's soul, but also to study the psychological effects of being in another person's body for so long.

So far, the prognosis doesn't look good.

The subject is depressed and angry. He begs me to die whenever I talk to him.

Will that be Willow's fate?

She already disapproves of using Eden's body, saying it ought to be properly buried, not be a tool of her father's.

I order donuts, hot cocoa for me, and coffee for Willow, then head back to the house wishing I could smell the donuts.

I fumble with my keys to unlock the front door, step inside, and see Ella sitting on the living room floor, watching cartoons.

"Where's Mommy?" I ask, surprised to see our daughter in the living room without supervision.

"Mommy won't wake up."

"What?" I ask, putting the donuts and coffee on the dining room table before making my way to our bedroom.

I open the door and step inside.

Willow is still in bed, covers pulled over her, just as I'd left her before sneaking out that morning.

I shake her, but she doesn't rouse.

A chill runs through me.

I pull the covers aside.

Her eyes are wide open.

Vomit on her lips and down her chin, on the pillow.

My stomach lurches as reality hits me like a train.

No, no, no, no.

I shake her again.

"Willow?"

She's cold, her skin almost blue.

"Is Mommy okay?" Ella asks, standing behind me.

No.

No.

No.

How long has she been dead?

I try to feel for a connection, some way to capture her soul if it isn't too late.

But there's nothing.

"Mommy?" Ella asks coming over to the bed and pushing her.

She giggles when she sees her mother's eyes open, thinking she's playing some game.

"Mommy," she says, "wake up."

When Willow doesn't move, Ella realizes something's wrong. Tears well in her eyes. "Mommy?"

I grab Ella, carry her back to the living room, and set her on the couch. "Sit here a minute, okay?"

She's crying, scared, confused.

I wonder if she has any concept of death.

I grab the phone and dial 9-1-1 even though I know it's too late.

Then I call Arnold. "She's … she's dead."

THE NEXT FEW hours pass in a flurry. Willow's mom keeps Ella occupied while the police *and* Arnold grill me.

How the hell did Willow overdose? How long had she been abusing the painkillers we found in her nightstand? And why didn't I say anything?

Yes, I knew she was depressed, but I don't think she was abusing drugs.

I have no answers.

I didn't see this coming.

Arnold is devastated, at one point yelling, "Everything I've done is now for nothing!" before storming out.

I'm left alone in the house, staring at the empty bed, my heart in countless pieces.

I rip off the sheets, pissed, and carry them to the washing machine.

I lift the lid, about to throw the sheets inside, when I see something taped to the interior lid.

A yellow envelope.

I drop the sheets and tear it open.

It's a letter in Willow's handwriting:

Dearest Ben,

I'm so sorry that I had to do it like this.

I'm even sorrier that I couldn't tell you, knowing you'd try to stop me.

The doctor told me that I have inoperable brain cancer. I might have a few months left, at best.

I know that would've given you time to do that thing you and my father were planning, but I can't let you.

There's something else I've learned in recent months, and again, it's something I didn't know how to tell you.

My father is not a good man.

If I let him put my soul into Eden's body, bad things would have happened.

I know the obvious question is WHAT sorts of bad things?

And that I can't tell you, other than to say the worst.

You can't trust him, Ben.

You need to find a way to distance yourself AND ELLA from my father before it's too late.

I'm sorry if it seems like I'm being vague, but I don't have better answers than that. I only know that I had to end things on my terms rather than becoming a pawn in what he's planning next.

Please tell Ella that I loved her more than she can ever know.

Please protect her from my father.

And thank you for saying yes to me despite knowing that you were agreeing to a tragedy.

I wish things could have worked out differently.

Perhaps we'll meet again in whatever's next.

❧

I LOVE YOU,
Willow Shepherd

❧

As I STAND HERE, tears flowing down my cheeks, all I can think is that we were supposed to have one more year.

One more year.

Chapter Sixteen

ELLA SHEPHERD AGE 7

I WAKE up to a weird blue nightlight brightening my walls.

I'm not a baby. I don't have a nightlight. Did Daddy put one in my room?

I look around and see that my posters are all gone, replaced with boy posters of football players and cars and superheroes.

At first, I think Daddy's playing a joke on me. But then I see other things that are different — the room is bigger, and so is my bed. The window and curtains are different. So is everything else.

I look around, scared, my eyes starting to water.

This isn't my room.

This isn't our home.

How did I get here?

Did someone kidnap me?

I jump out of bed and run to the bedroom door that isn't mine.

I open it.

I'm in a big house I've never seen. It's two stories.

I run downstairs, not knowing where to go.

But I can't stay. I'm not supposed to be here.

I need to find a phone.

I need to call the police and then Daddy.

I go into the kitchen looking for a phone on the wall like some houses still have, but I don't see one.

No!

I look outside the kitchen window. Outside it's dark and scary.

I don't know what to do. Do I go outside and look until I find someone with a phone? Or do I go upstairs and see if whoever lives here has a mobile?

I start to go outside, but a dog barks in the yard and scares me.

I could go out the front door instead, but what if the dog isn't on a leash or behind a gate?

I go back upstairs and peek inside the only open doors in sight. One is a bathroom, and the other is an office like Daddy's at home.

I go inside, looking for a phone.

I find one on the desk.

I pick it up. It's different from Daddy's, but I'm guessing it turns on the same way.

I push the button at the bottom of the screen.

The screen asks me for a passcode.

No!

I start to press numbers, hoping I might be lucky enough to guess the right one.

Then the phone says it's blocked.

No!

A light comes on.

A fat woman is standing in her pajamas, looking at me.

"Honey, why are you up?"

"Who are you?" I ask.

But my voice doesn't sound like my voice.

It sounds like a boy's.

What's going on?

"I've gotta go to the bathroom," I say, rushing past her, into the bathroom.

I flip on the light and look in the mirror.

Instead of me, I see a brown-skinned boy about six years old.

What is going on?

I scream.

"Honey?" the woman asks grabbing me, tight.

No!

I've got to get away.

Got to go downstairs and run out the front door, dogs or not.

Got to find a phone that I can use to call Daddy.

"Let me go!" I yell, kicking, thrashing.

The woman holds me tight, crying, "What's wrong, honey?"

"I'm not your honey!" I yell, kicking her hard in the leg.

She finally lets go.

I run towards the stairs, turn, grabbing the rail, trying to right myself before I hit the top step.

Instead, my hand slips and I fly right over the rail.

THEN I'M BACK in my bed, screaming.

Dad runs in. "What's wrong, Ella?"

"I don't know!" I cry out as he holds me.

I feel better in his arms, but not yet safe.

What happened to me?

Who was that boy?

Was I really in that house?

"Daddy, I need to tell you something you might not believe."

"What is it, Ella?"

"You *havta* promise that you'll believe me."

"I promise."

"I think I was in someone else's body."

Chapter Seventeen

Ben Shepherd Age 28

ELLA RELATES HER EXPERIENCE, and I tell her that she's probably sick. Sometimes people hallucinate when they're ill.

Please don't let her be one.

Please, God.

I have to keep the fear from showing. She's hyper-intuitive, just like her mother. It makes lying impossible. I've always suspected that she might be a touch psychic and could read minds, even though she's never said anything to prove it.

But what if her gift is Jumping?

I don't know what to do.

Should I tell her what I know?

That sounds awful, especially since I barely know anything.

And while I know that AD was trying to start a Jumper program, I don't know if they ever got it off the ground.

I think of Eden Jumping and never returning. Now she's a damned robot.

"Are you okay, Daddy?" Ella asks.

"Yeah, yeah, just trying to decide what to do about school. I think you need to stay home."

"But I don't feel sick."

Ella is one of those odd children who hates staying home and looks forward to school.

"Yeah, but sometimes you don't realize you're sick. Let me call my work and tell them that I'm not coming in."

I bring Ella to the living room, scatter her stuffies on the couch all around her, along with her favorite pillows and blankets, then I find something she can watch on TV.

I go into my home office, keeping the door open.

I scan the local news websites and find a story about a young boy who fell down the stairs last night. He's in intensive care. His mother told police that her son woke up screaming. The things he said match what Ella described to me.

Shit.

I deeply sigh as I pick up my phone to make a horrifying call.

A call that Willow would kill me if she knew I was making.

But who else can I turn to but Arnold Fairchild?

I haven't seen him since Willow's funeral.

I moved out of his guest house and quit working at AD.

He wasn't happy, said I was ruining so many things by leaving. That you just don't abandon a project when the going gets rough.

I told him this wasn't about the "going getting rough"

but rather about my daughter — *his granddaughter* — needing me more than him.

He wasn't happy, but he didn't press hard after the Ella card was played.

I still had money from my father's insurance, so I found an apartment a few hours away and started doing some freelance handyman work at an old folk's community nearby. We're not rich, but we're doing fine.

And I'm home every night for my daughter.

It's a life free from Deviant drama. Or at least it was.

Now that Ella has Jumped, everything's changed.

I dial Fairchild's number.

"Well, well, well," he answers. "I thought I'd never hear from you again."

"We need to talk, Mr. Fairchild. About Ella."

Chapter Eighteen

Ben Shepherd Age 28

AFTER KOTKE and the doctors evaluate Ella, her grandmother shows up, wanting to eat lunch with her granddaughter whom she hasn't seen since we moved away.

"Oh my God, you've grown so big. Are you sure you're only seven?"

She scoops Ella into a hug, then shoots me an accusatory glance while embracing my daughter.

I wish I could tell her that I've not been around because Willow warned me away from Arnold. But that probably wouldn't go over well.

And right now, I need her husband's expertise to prevent Ella from Jumping into The Void and getting sucked up by a Collector.

As the ladies head to the cafeteria, Fairchild pulls me aside into his private library.

"Brandy?" he asks, pouring himself a drink.

"No," I say.

"Please, sit." He waves toward the love seat that Willow and I sat in so many years ago.

"So," he starts right in, not wasting any time, "why did you leave? I dare guess that it isn't so you can fulfill your lifelong dream of being a handyman?"

"I already told you that I want to be with Ella. She's lost her mother. She deserves as much of my time as I can give her."

"You could've given her all the time you wanted if you stayed at AD. Plus, you wouldn't need to worry about money or housing. You could move right back into the guest house and always have a babysitter on hand."

"I'm happy where I am. *We're* happy where we are."

He looks at me with his skeptical eyes, sips his brandy, then sets it on the end table next to his chair. "She told you to stay away, didn't she?"

"What?" I act confused, wondering if he's prying into my mind. Is he so good that I wouldn't even be able to catch him snooping?

"Please, don't insult my intelligence, Ben. I know Willow wasn't happy with certain projects we're working on."

"She never discussed her work."

"Really?" Arnold asks, eyebrows arched.

I meet his gaze straight, not needing to lie. "We only talked about work when I updated her on the projects involving our attempts to save her. But she never told me anything about the stuff she was doing."

He smiles.

I think he believes me.

"I just find it odd that you not only quit your job, you never come by with our grandchild. Not in five years.

Seems damned ungrateful to the man who treated you like a son, took you in when your father went nuts and shot at a bunch of cops."

Anger burns through my veins. How dare he bring up my father?

"Fine, you want the truth? Willow killed herself."

He doesn't say a word. Not even the arch of an eyebrow.

I'm surprised that he doesn't seem surprised.

"Did she leave a letter?"

"Yes."

"What did it say?"

I tell him, not even sure why other than it feels liberating to do so after all this time. And I want him to hurt like I do.

I've spent five years hating Fairchild for his role in Willow's death, even if I don't know his exact level of responsibility. I just find it hard not to blame him when his daughter would rather take her own life than be part of whatever secret shit he's been into.

He downs the rest of his brandy then sighs, leaning back in his chair. "Do you want to know why Willow was afraid?"

"I do."

"Fine. But first some background on AD. My father, Charles Fairchild, was a doctor in the second World War, among the first to liberate Auschwitz. You've heard about the horrible medical experiments they did there, right?"

I nod.

"Well, there were also other secret experiments that the public never knew about. Orphanages where doctors experimented on Deviants, trying to figure out why they had powers, and how they could gain those abilities for themselves. They had a battery of plans, from improving the Aryan race to creating true super soldiers.

"One of the older orphans was a Jewish Deviant named Lena. She and her twin sister suffered terribly from the experiments. Her sister died during the experiments. Lena was a powerful psychic and telepath. Yet she never used her powers to escape because she was afraid of what the Nazis would do to her friends. She worked closely with a couple of doctors who were trying to breed the right kind of soldier. They forced other Deviants to rape her, hoping they could mix one type of power with another to create boutique Deviants. Like breeding dogs. Starting at age thirteen, she had six children at the orphanage, each of them dying either through sickness or murder when they didn't have the right powers.

"You never heard about these orphanages or the Deviants because the Americans made a deal with the Nazi doctors to bring their work, and their orphans, over to the States as part of Operation Paperclip. The States would've signed a deal with Satan himself if it gave them a one-up on the Russians.

"My father was brought on because of three things: his medical background, his trustworthiness, and because he was the only one Lena would talk to. They worked for the CIA for a while, and eventually fell in love and got married. Lena never thought any man would marry her because the sick experiments turned her barren. But Charles didn't care if he had kids or not. He only cared about Lena, the love of his life.

"Decades passed, and things were going okay. Then, one day, out of the blue, Lena got pregnant, with me. This should've been the happiest day of my parents' lives. But it turns out that my birth was a curse and my mother died in labor.

I sit there, stunned. "Willow never told me any of this."

"It's not her story to tell," Arnold continued. "Anyway, my father began to treat me more like an experiment than a child, working with the Top Secret program, alongside Nazi doctors who were still alive and unpunished for their crimes, trying to turn me into a super soldier."

"Jesus. And?"

"Honestly, I didn't mind. Dad said we were doing the Lord's work, looking for ways to protect the nation against its enemies. For a while, I served as a spy and an interrogator. I was damned good at my job. Eventually, the government created AD, a legitimate research group operating as a front for our CIA black book projects. After I left the field, I came to work here, working my way to Director."

"So, are you still running those Nazi experiments?"

"God no, Ben. We're working to stop the bad guys. To stop terrorists. To stop people like Hitler from ever taking power again."

"So why didn't Willow want to be part of that? It sounds like good work."

"It is, but we had a difference of opinion about one of my key programs, Project Karma."

"What's that?"

"What if I told you we have already thwarted major terrorist attacks? Not just once, but hundreds of times."

"*Hundreds?*"

"Hundreds."

"How?"

"It's one thing to get a vision of something horrible that's about to happen. It's quite another when we can get a vision of something that we can stop *before it even happens*. Using Eden's visions, we pair a seer like Willow with a Jumper. Together they can leap into the bad guys, spy, then neutralize them to prevent atrocities and save the world from evil before it can strike. The best part is that there's no danger to the Jumper. If they die inside another body, they'll wake up back in their own."

I don't get into the theoretical weeds, like asking how they can justify neutralizing an enemy that hasn't yet attempted to act. Or how while there's no danger to the Jumper, there is for the people they're Jumping into. Instead, I say, "I thought you hadn't perfected Jumping? What if you have another accident, like with Eden?"

"We've perfected it, Ben. We now have three pairs of Jumpers and co-pilots protecting the world every day."

"If it's so safe then why didn't Willow want to be involved?"

"Because about six months after Ella was born, she had a vision that showed Ella working with us. And she didn't want it. She doesn't want her child fighting grown-up wars."

"Well, neither do I."

"And I understand that. In truth, we don't even need Ella. As I said, we have three pairs, and they're doing great work. It's a shame that Willow killed herself trying to stop something that wasn't ever going to happen."

"You're saying you wouldn't let Ella work with the program?"

"I'd always defer to your judgment, Ben."

I sense no duplicity in his response. I sigh, "To be fair, I didn't know about any of this."

I feel like an ass, like I'm throwing Willow under the bus or something, minimizing her fears. But Fairchild, or at least the Academy, might be Ella's only hope in learning to control her ability, and I need to keep Ella's options open, despite Willow's or my feelings for the old man.

"Of course." Fairchild nods. "This must all feel like a ton of bricks landing on you."

He gets up to refresh his glass. "You sure you don't want one?"

"I'm tired, I'm stressed, and I'm scared shitless that my daughter will Jump and never come back. So, yeah, I'd like a drink, thank you."

He pours me a drink and hands it to me.

"Ella doesn't have to be in danger. We can help her."

I sip my drink then meet his gaze, trying to size up the offer. He seems sincere, and, when it comes down to it, what choice do I have?

"What can you do for her?"

"Teach her to harness her power. Control where she Jumps and how to Jump back."

"And what if I won't allow it? What'll happen to Ella then?"

He shakes his head. "I don't think either one of us wants to contemplate that. Do we?"

"No," I say, wondering if I'm making a deal with the devil.

Chapter Nineteen

Ella Shepherd Age 13

I HOP out of the Jumping Chamber eager to tell Eden what I learned while in the Senator's body.

But Penelope, the lady who runs the Jumping Program, makes me lie down on her exam table first.

"Come on. I need to debrief."

"Not yet," she says. "We need to check your vitals first. I won't have your dad come down here raising hell."

Dad can be such a pain in the butt. He means well, but he's overly cautious about *everything*.

"I like your hair like that," I say.

Penelope is wearing her dark hair in pigtails today. She's in her late twenties, and the coolest adult by far. While most of the others wear lab outfits or suits, Penelope dresses more like me, in jeans, shirts, and the occasional duster. I also love her bright blue wireframe glasses.

"Thank you," she says, slipping the blood pressure cuff

over my arm. "It won't take long. I just need to submit the report that you're okay."

"Do you also put the stuff about the Senator in there?"

"No, because your grandfather issues that job to you, not me. And I'd rather have your dad mad at me than him."

I smile. "Don't worry. My Dad won't find out. It's just a little harmless spying."

"Don't tell me anything. Plausible deniability and all."

"Fine, fine, if you don't want to know who the Senator is sleeping with."

"Stop it!" Penelope shakes her head. "I'm here to supervise your Jumps, not collect top secret info."

"Fine."

She checks me head to toe, then says, "Okay, good to go."

"Bye," I say, skipping out the door, then down the hall to Eden's room.

I know she isn't human, that Eden is a super computer or something like that, but talking to her still makes me miss my mom a little less.

Eden's office is all white, two chairs on either side of an eggshell table in the center of the room. Mirrors surround us, save for the door.

I always feel watched here, but what can I do? This whole place is monitored. I have to deal with it. At least if I want to Jump. And I do.

I love Jumping, and I'm good at it. Grandfather thinks I'm the best he's ever had. I can't go on dangerous missions yet, but he says that once I'm eighteen, I won't need my father's permission. He said it was best not to mention that unless I wanted Dad to get mad and pull me out of the program now.

Eden is the only person I can share my Jumping stories

with, other than Serena, the psychic I'm paired with. But I don't get to talk with her much since she's usually paired with another Jumper named Kat.

"Good afternoon, Ella," Eden greets me.

"Hello, Eden. How are you?"

"I'm fine. Would you like some small talk before your debriefing?"

"Sheesh, can't you be a bit more human? People don't say it like that, *Hello, Eden. Would you like some small talk before your debriefing?*" I mimic her, making her voice sound more robotic than it is.

Eden laughs.

I wonder if she truly finds me funny or if it's part of her programming, the AI's attempt to appear more human.

"Sorry, how should I respond?"

"I dunno, maybe *any other way than you did?*"

"Should we start over?"

"Yes," I say, popping out of my seat, going out the door, then coming back in. "Hi, Eden, how's it going?"

"There was a fire in an Indian textile today that killed more than one hundred employees."

"Jesus, *that's* your idea of small talk?"

Eden stares at me for a long moment, then bursts out laughing. "Was I funny?"

I laugh. "Yes, Eden. Yes, that was funny. Well, as funny as a tragedy can be."

I fill her in on all the stuff I learned about Senator Williams. After I've spilled everything, I lean forward and whisper, just in case we're being watched. "What do they do with this information?"

"I run it through my database, comparing it with collected information and predictions from the psychics to determine the best course of action, whether that be a Jumper intervening or something else."

"*You* determine the course of action?"

"Don't let my appearance fool you, Ella. I'm far more advanced than anything the world has ever seen."

"Wow," I say, truly in awe. "Is it because you're part human?"

She nods. "That, and because of Eden's abilities."

"She was a Deviant?"

"Yes."

"What was her power?" I've asked Dad a few times how Eden died, but he's never told me. He always insists that it's classified.

"She Jumped, and her body died before her soul could return."

I swallow. "That can happen?"

Eden nods. "Yes."

"How many times has it happened?"

"There are four known instances."

I'm guessing that Eden senses my fear. She reaches out to touch my hand. "You needn't worry. The technology has been perfected. And you're all in the Jump Chambers which monitor your vitals. If anything were to happen to your body during the Jump, we'd pull you right back."

"Right back into a dying body? What if someone didn't want to be pulled back just to die? What if they preferred to stay out there as a Jumper, borrowing bodies but living forever?"

"I don't know. That's something you'd have to discuss with Mr. Fairchild." Then after a long moment, Eden adds, "Why? Is that what you'd want? To live forever?"

"I dunno. It might be kinda cool."

She smiles. "Yes, it might be."

❧

Two weeks later...

❧

As I'M WALKING to my usual Jump Chamber — in another wing than the full-timers use — Penelope pulls me aside.

"Change of plans, Ella Belle."

"What?"

"Come with me."

She leads me through the chamber, down a hall, then to the elevators, descending another level.

She brings me to a room with two exam tables.

Eden is lying on one, looking at me.

"Hello, Ella. How 'bout those Indian textiles?"

I laugh.

Penelope looks at me, eyebrows arched. "Huh?"

"Inside joke."

"Ah. Okay, so here's the deal. Eden was thinking about what you said in one of your meetings, about wanting to live forever. She'd like to start copying your brain."

"You can copy a brain?"

Penelope says, "I'll let her explain it. I'm going to leave you here. Come and see me when you're done."

I want to tell her to wait, to please come back. I haven't even agreed to have my brain copied, and she's acting like I have.

But she's gone before I can object.

Eden sits up, explaining, "Yes, we can copy your brain with the intention of later uploading it to a substrate."

"A what?"

"Just a fancy word for a storage spot for your brain. It

can be a computer, a robot, or, in your case, another human."

"So I'd be able to live *forever?*"

"Well, not technically. It would be a copy of your brain. Your actual consciousness resides in your soul. However, if we could upload both your soul and a copy of your brain to the same substrate, you could live forever. It's what they were planning to do with your mother before she died."

"My Dad told me a bit about it, but not … wait. Are you saying that I'm going to die?"

"All humans die eventually. But you don't have to."

"Do you know something that I don't? Did one of the psychics see me dying?"

"No, Ella. I simply wanted to offer you the option of living forever."

"Why?"

"Because I like you."

"No offense, but it feels weird hearing you say that you *like* me. You're a computer, can a computer *like* someone?"

"Are you asking if I have feelings?"

"Yes."

"Well then, yes, of course I do. Though someone made me, and I'm very advanced, I'm not all that different from you. Everything you do and think and feel — all of it comes down to simple electrical impulses. I'm programmed to be as human in those ways as you are."

I stare at Eden, feeling a deeper sense of kinship. I've liked her for a long time. In many ways, she's been the sister I never had. Though I don't know how she has so many stories about my mother, I love every one of them.

I used to feel weird thinking of her like that, but now that she's reduced our similarities to electrical impulses, I suppose it doesn't feel that much different than having the same feelings for a person.

Eden continues, "In the years before your mom died, we spent a lot of time together. As you know, she was going to live inside me. But when she passed before that could happen, I deeply felt the loss."

"You did?"

"Yes. And after she died and your father went away, I missed him, too. I felt terrible that the one thing he wanted, to put your mother's soul inside me, he never got a chance to do."

She pauses, her eyes watering.

"Oh my God, you can cry?"

She wipes at her eyes. "If I can feel, I can cry."

"Oh, my God." Not knowing she had feelings, I never considered how sad it must've been for her after my mother's death. "Can I hug you?"

"I would like that."

I hug Eden as we cry.

We let go, and she asks, "So, do you want to live forever?"

"Yes," I say.

"Then let's get started."

Chapter Twenty

Ben Shepherd Age 36

I'M SITTING in my office at The Academy for Talent and Distinction, going through the latest updates of kids I've recruited when there's a buzz from my secretary, James.

"There's a student here to see you, sir. Irina Pochenko."

I look at my computer. I don't have any appointments scheduled this morning. It's almost noon, and I promised Ella that we'd eat lunch together. She doesn't have many friends and spends way too much time with that damned cyborg, Eden. I figured we could go into town and have a nice long lunch, if only to give her — both of us, really — some semblance of normalcy. Some much-needed daddy daughter time.

I'm almost always working out of town these days. And when I'm here, Ella tends to be a moody teenager, not wanting to talk.

I told myself I'd work less when I came back with her.

And, for a while, I did, toiling with Kotke on the random project, but keeping my nights and weekends free for Ella.

But Fairchild asked me to take over for an ill recruiter a few years ago, and that meant working with Eden again, something I'd been trying to avoid.

But a job is a job, and to be honest, I was becoming ever more curious about Eden's growing powers, especially after hearing so much about them from Ella and Kotke.

Not only were Eden's psychic abilities constantly growing stronger, but she's also Jumping, something we didn't even think was possible without a soul. Fairchild argues that this thing that he's created is perhaps a new kind of soul.

I don't see how anything manmade can be a soul, but whatever it is, the thing is Jumping into the world every night, casting a net, searching for Deviants.

She finds Deviants with strong auras. She spies on them to see if they're good candidates and if we can find the right leverage so I can get the parents to send their kid to a "special school for gifted students."

Many parents think I'm high, asking some variation of "you think my kid is special?" A lot of them think their kids are a handful and are perfectly happy to have anyone, particularly a school in the northwest, take their kid for months at a time.

Many of the kids don't even have parents.

And somehow recruiting has become a twenty-four seven job that keeps me on the road more often than not.

I tell myself that it's okay, that Ella is fine, that she doesn't even need me that much these days. She's a teenager, after all.

But these other kids, Deviants, many who come from

bad situations — orphans and foster kids, troubled children whose parents don't know what to do with them or understand their special needs — require my attention. Especially when they first arrive and have yet to form a bond with any of our counselors.

I'm the only adult they've spoken with, so they come to me with their problems. It's mostly the usual stuff: fitting in, some bullying, peer pressure, loneliness, but amped past ten because most of these kids have *always* felt like outcasts.

They've grown up not understanding why they were different, behind a lifetime of being told to bury their abilities. We usually get them before their powers truly develop, before they bring unwanted attention to themselves from others. Or worse, the media. Despite living mostly under the radar, they've always known they were different. And they were bullied for any perceived difference.

So many of our recruits carry that baggage, finding it difficult to fit in, especially when they're going to classes and living with second, third, and fourth generation Deviants who more or less grew up at the Academy and occupy the top rung of the school's social ladder. There is always a hierarchy, even on a campus of misfits.

Human nature never fails to fuck up a good thing. People always find a way to instill a pecking order, to ensure there's someone at the bottom, someone to keep down if only to prop themselves up.

So while I'm *not* a counselor, I'm more of a counselor than the ones here paid to do that job.

I look at the clock and figure I've got fifteen minutes.

"Okay, send her in," I tell James.

Moments later, Irina enters.

I recruited Irina and her twin brother, Nikolai, three years ago from a foster family. It was a bad situation, a couple of assholes had a house filled with neglected kids.

They were obviously doing it just for the money, making me question the foster care system and humanity in general.

Irina and Niko weren't just neglected; they were picked on by the other foster kids who made fun of their thick Russian accents and naïveté.

The school paid off the foster family and some government officials to let us raise the kids.

And things were going okay, until The Incident six months ago, which cost a student his life during a training exercise.

After that, Niko went to Aspen Falls Psychiatric Hospital, a AD division where we keep the most dangerous Deviants.

Irina steps into my office and takes a seat in an overstuffed leather chair in front of my desk. Her eyes are bloodshot. Her nose is red.

"I need your help, Mr. Shepherd," she says in her Russian accent.

"What's wrong?"

"My brother, Niko, something's wrong, and nobody will tell me anything."

She proceeds to tell me that a month ago or so she stopped sensing her brother. They used to communicate telepathically, even after he went to the hospital. Even when they couldn't *talk*, she could always sense him. But it's been four weeks, and she hasn't felt a thing.

Irina had asked her assigned counselor Morgan Mathews if Niko was okay. Two days later Morgan told her that yes, Irina's brother was fine. But when she asked to see Niko, something she'd been able to do once a month since his admission to the hospital, Irina was told that Niko was on lockdown.

The counselor didn't give any other details, and Irina

has been growing increasingly afraid that something awful has happened.

"I don't think he's coming back," she says, arms folded across her chest, chin quivering as she battles her tears. "I think he's dead."

"I'm sure he's not dead," I say, even though I'm not sure. "I would've heard something. Maybe they have him on some medications or something that's dampening his connection?"

Irina and Niko both have telepathic and telekinetic abilities, but Niko is far more powerful, with a third ability that came online right before he was put into the hospital — a vampiric touch that absorbs the abilities of anyone he comes into contact with, while also draining that person's life force.

I wonder if he's proved so dangerous that they're drugging him up. Or maybe he's being kept in a chamber which is scrambling his ability to send or receive signals. We've found that continuous noise and some radio signals work well to interfere with telepaths.

"I'll make some calls and see what I can find out."

Irina stares at me then lets out a long sigh before finally getting her question out. "My brother is gone a month, and you don't keep in touch to see how he is? I thought you were supposed to be looking out for us."

"I do look out for you all, but I don't work at the hospital."

"But you have access, right? You could have found out how he was. Why didn't you?"

Do I tell her the truth, that with so many kids to keep track of, including my own, I don't have time to worry about her brother?

The truth is that while Niko has very much been an ongoing discussion among both co-workers and Fairchild in our weekend dinners, those conversations have always been more about his victim, a third generation nineteen-year-old Deviant girl named Ryo. She had incredible strength and was one of the key people Fairchild was building a military project around. But now Ryo was dead, and her family devastated.

Fairchild was more concerned with fallout from the girl's death than Niko's mental well-being.

And I, well, I'd never even thought of checking in on the boy.

"I'm sorry," I say. "You're right. I should've checked in on him."

She stares at me, and I can't read her emotion.

I wonder if she's trying to pry inside my head to see if I'm holding something back. If she is, I can't sense her prying. And my psychic defenses are among the best.

"I'll make some calls today," I say again.

She's still staring at me.

"I promise."

Irina stands, "Thank you, Mr. Shepherd."

She looks down at her feet as she leaves my office.

I stare at the door as it swings shut, then pick up the phone and call Kotke.

He picks up, and I hear the wind on his side of the call — he must be walking somewhere for lunch.

"Irina Pochenko was just in my office asking about her brother. Do you know what's going on with him?"

"What's she asking?"

His non-answer confirms that something is wrong. The knot in my stomach promises that this day is about to get a whole lot worse.

I answer his question with another of my own.

"What happened?"

"Damn," he says with a dramatic sigh. "I was *trying* to

get in a couple of miles on my lunch."

"Where are you?" I ask, even though the last thing I feel like doing is jogging. "I'll come with you."

"No, it's better if we talk in my office."

～

I CALL Ella to ask if we can meet for dinner instead.

She sighs — I'm getting a lot of sighs today — then says, "Yeah, whatever," before hanging up.

I meet with Kotke in his lab. Despite being at least two dozen years older than me, he still looks dapper as ever, even wearing workout clothes. His white hair is still full, and his face almost wrinkle-free.

He locks the doors, then leads me into the back of the room, into his private office and looks at me. "What did she ask?"

"She wants to know if her brother is alive. Says she's been asking to see him, but they said he's on lockdown. She thinks he might be dead."

"Why would she say that?"

"Because she can't feel him. So, what the hell is going on?"

"Your father-in-law hasn't told you anything?"

"No. Last I knew, Niko was in Aspen Falls after what happened with Ryo."

"Then I probably shouldn't say anything."

"Come on, don't make me go out to the old man's house this weekend. I was looking forward to time with just me and Ella. I wanted to take her hiking."

"Okay, but if he asks, I didn't tell you."

"Fine."

"They never stopped Project Iron Knuckles after Ryo's death."

"Wasn't it dependent on Ryo?"

"Now Niko has her powers. They transferred testing to a more controlled environment — the chambers at The Lighthouse, with the Fours and Fives."

"So, he's not at Aspen Falls?"

"He was there, briefly, before they moved him to The Lighthouse."

Before we take in a new Deviant, we determine their placement. Most non-violent Deviants are considered Levels One through Three. Those capable of some serious damage are considered Levels Four and Five.

Fours and Fives are sent to The Lighthouse, a sister school next to Aspen Falls. It's a more regimented place, where kids are basically on lockdown. While our Ones, Twos, and Threes will likely eventually work in intelligence, either with the FBI, the CIA, or the AD division, Fours and Fives will be steered down a different career path — black ops soldiers working off the radar, killing enemies of the state.

That was Ryo's path.

But Niko isn't Ryo.

"So, we're turning him into a killer for the agency?"

"Fairchild doesn't like setbacks. And getting Project Iron Knuckles up and running is priority number one if we expect to keep our funding."

"Jesus." I'm pacing, trying to come to terms with what Kotke is saying. "This is fucked up. Niko is only a kid!"

Kotke quotes Fairchild: "The wheels of progress wait for no man."

Most of our graduates are involved in long distance warfare like psychic spying, or they're trained well — for years — with the best military fighters around before their first black ops mission. Sending a kid into battle is beyond the pale.

"Did something happen to Niko after he went to The Lighthouse?"

"Yes," Kotke says. "About a month ago, Niko was training, a standard exercise against some other Fours and Fives, when he suffered a heart attack. Medics administered CPR and paddles, trying to bring him back, but nothing was working. He was dead."

"*Was* dead?"

"Yes. *Was.* One of our subjects in the room at the time, a telepath, saw a Collector coming to claim Niko's soul."

I lean forward, remembering my interaction with the Collector who took my father, and how I briefly saw through its eyes.

A chill runs through me.

"But when The Collector went to coax Niko's soul from his body, Niko suddenly shot up, wide awake. And The Collector fell to the ground before vanishing."

"What are you saying?"

"Niko came back. And it seems like he took The Collector's soul. *And its powers.*"

I stare, shocked. "How can that even happen? They—"

"We don't know." Kotke shakes his head. "But Fairchild is shifting gears on the project as we speak. Niko was just upgraded to a Level Seven."

I wasn't even aware of a Level beyond Six, and there are only a few known Sixes in the world. Of those, all are locked up in Aspen Falls because they've lost their minds.

Kotke continues, "He came back from the dead. He not only takes powers now, but he takes souls."

"Wait a second. He took someone's soul? Why the hell are they letting anyone near him?"

"*Let?* Hell, it was like feeding a lion. They threw some crazy patient in there with him, forced the guy to defend himself. Then when he did, Niko took the guy's soul."

"And then what?" I ask, afraid to know more, barely able to believe what I'm hearing.

Fairchild has ordered people to do some questionable things in the past, but murdering a patient? The fact that Kotke says this so matter-of-factly makes me wonder how much more AD does that I'm in the dark about.

"Niko vanished for eleven minutes, then came back, saying he'd gone to The Void. Then, just like that, he was back at the hospital. And he didn't remember a thing that happened during this time in The Void."

I can't even imagine what the hell Fairchild is planning to do with Niko now. I don't want to know because I'm sure it will send me off the deep end.

I look at Kotke. "Have you seen Niko since all this?"

"Yeah, I've run some tests."

"And?"

"He's … changed."

"How?"

"For one, he's a lot quieter. Traumatized. For two, his aura, his signature, is all wrong. It isn't human. And third, he can't remember much before The Collector touched him. It was like it reset something inside him."

"Is that why his sister can't reach him?"

"He's on lockdown until they know more about what they're dealing with. It isn't safe for her to be near him. And we need to keep this top secret. That means that Irina can't know."

"What the hell am I supposed to tell her?"

He pauses for a long time, perhaps considering the question. Is Kotke as troubled by all of this as I am? Or is he used to executing Fairchild's questionable methods to fulfill the AD agenda?

He finally responds. "Tell her that he's dead."

I stare at Kotke in disbelief "No. I'm not lying to her."

"What then? Tell her the truth? Why do that? Why torment her? She'll never be able to see him again. He's Level Seven, Ben. Nobody can see him without clearance."

"Maybe things will change. Maybe his level will come down."

"That's not how it works, Ben. I get it, you're an optimist, and you've preferred to keep yourself out of all the Project stuff, including your own daughter's work, but when it comes to Level Seven … that's as hardcore as it gets. We couldn't even let Irina see her brother if I thought it was a great idea, which I don't."

I shake my head, disgusted with the situation, and that nobody said anything to Irina before now. Why should this fall on me to handle? Why expect *me* to lie to her?

I head out of the office hating my job.

I RETURN to the admin building to find Irina waiting in the lobby outside my office, sitting in a chair opposite James, who is busy talking to someone on the phone. Probably a parent requesting a meeting.

Irina stands the second she sees me. "What did you find out, Mr. Shepherd?"

"Come," I say, nodding at James as I open my office door.

Irina steps through and takes a seat in front of my desk.

I close my door and trudge toward my desk, steeling myself for a lie that I don't want to tell.

I sit, then look up at Irina.

Before I can utter a word, I feel her in my head.

I try to push her out, but she's in so fast, I can't prepare a psychic defense.

"Stop," I say.

Irina says nothing.

I can feel her rooting through my memories. Even though I don't want them to, I can feel my words with Kotke, along with my emotional reaction to them, playing out in my head.

When did she get so good at intrusion?

Then I hear her voice in my head.

"My brother always told me never to let anyone know my true limits. That it's always better to let people underestimate you."

Shit. Irina is at least a Level Four if she can get past my defenses. She's glaring at me.

"You were going to tell me he died?"

"It's for the best."

"Best for whom?"

She stands up, about to head for the door.

"No," I say, grabbing her arm.

Time freezes. She glances up at me, her eyes boring into mine. Forget Level Four, the girl is Level Six, minimum.

As I stare into her eyes, I realize I have no clue what she's capable of, or how far she might go in a fit of anger.

I could defend myself. I've kept up with my training, so I could blast her with energy, overload her with data, shut down her brain, or even create a high-pitched digital scream from all the nearby electronic equipment that would incapacitate her.

But I don't want to hurt her.

She's just a kid.

I let go and say, "Please, hear me out."

"What?" Her arms are crossed, her foot tapping.

"I'm not sure what you plan to do, but you can't let them know that you know."

"Why?"

"You saw my memories. And surely, you know what Kotke said. You're not cleared."

"I'll let them know how powerful I am. They'll have to let me in with him!"

"You still won't get clearance. Not for Level Seven. Trust me. They won't let you see him."

"I'm not giving them a choice," she says, pushing her way past me. "I'm *going* to see him."

I reach out to grab her again, but she spins, quickly, and grabs my hand with hers.

And as we connect, a spark.

And then, all around me, the world is filled with a high-pitched digital shrieking.

I fall to the ground, covering my ears.

Irina runs out of the office.

And then I realize that she has the same gift as her brother.

She copied my powers.

I GO to the window to watch as Irina flees my office, heading toward the front gate.

She's leaving.

What the hell does she think she's doing? Does she really think she can just walk into Aspen Falls and demand to see her brother? She's going to get herself killed.

I consider running after her, but Irina doesn't want to hear me. She won't listen to logic. I have no choice but to make a call before she screws up her entire life.

I call the front gate. "We've got a Code Nine."

After giving them details so they can capture Irina without harming her, I call Fairchild.

"We've got a problem."

Chapter Twenty-One

ELLA SHEPHERD AGE 17

I'M SITTING in the breakroom just off the Jump Hangar eating lunch with my psychic Co-Pilot, Anders, a remote viewer who is among the best and youngest. We're waiting for Eden to arrive with today's Jump plans.

Anders is blind. My age, tall with long dark hair and giant shades that hide his eyes. He was born with flesh covering his sockets. I was pretty freaked out the first time I saw him. Before I got used to it. Still, I can see why he wears the shades. I'm sure he can sense the unease. And he's the kind of kid that wants to disappear, not be the subject of stares, whispers, and speculation.

He goes to my school, though we don't talk much outside of these pre-Jumps. We don't have classes together. He spends lunch with one of his three other male friends, or sometimes his twin sister, Alice. She was born with the same condition and is also a Jumper.

Anders used to Jump with Alice until I was brought into the program and we were paired together. Though neither of them has said anything to me, I feel like maybe she's upset that I was placed with her brother — not that I requested it.

In many ways, Anders feels like the brother I never had.

The connection between a Jumper and Pilot is special. We've made more than a hundred Jumps together. Each time he's in my head, guiding me, talking to me, seeing and feeling the same things that I am.

We may not talk much at school, but our bond runs deeper than anything I've felt outside my connections with Eden.

But unlike Eden, Anders can't just run through my head peeking in at my memories. Nor I his. It's more like we're sharing a car, and only privy to what's happening around us and the host body. He can see the memories as I go through them, which has given us many shared lifetimes.

We've experienced our hosts' loves, losses, adventures, and scares, vicariously living lives of the rich and powerful as well as people barely surviving on the fringes. And though we've never dared to discuss it, we've experienced sex as both men and women, together.

My first time was last year. Anders was right there with me.

It's weird to have gone through so much with one person but not even really know them in the real world.

In many ways, I suppose the real world pales compared to Jumping and living through others. I'd never tell my father because he already worries too much about everything, but I often prefer almost any life to my own.

Dad is working all the time, though it's always been like that.

I have no real friends at school. I don't connect with anyone. The scary thing is, I don't *want* to connect. Or make friends. Everyone says you're supposed to fall in love, but I don't want a boyfriend, either.

I like living as other people.

I look at Anders. He's barely touching his salad.

"What's wrong?" I ask.

"I don't know."

"You know something."

I actually mean it. The guy is psychic.

"You'll think I'm stupid."

"I already do," I joke.

Thankfully he laughs.

"Do you ever get scared when you're Jumping?"

"Scared? Of what?"

"That you might not come back. Like with Eden."

"It hasn't happened since Eden. So, no. Why? You know something I don't? Did you see something?"

"No."

"Then what is it?"

"I've been having these nightmares about losing you."

I lean forward. "Nightmares or visions?"

"They're not visions. They're different. I think."

"Did you tell anyone?" I look around, but we're still alone.

"No. But I probably should."

"Don't. They'll ground me for months until they think it's safe again."

He nods. "Yeah, probably."

I sip my water, staring at Anders, trying to determine if he's holding something back. I feel like he is, but it's hard to read someone without eyes.

Then we're no longer alone.

Eden arrives, carrying a tablet with my grandfather beside her.

"Hello, honey," he says coming over to hug me.

"Hi, Ella, Anders," Eden says. "Mr. Fairchild is here to monitor this very special mission."

This is the first time since the early days that Grandfather has been here for one of my Jumps. I'm not sure if I should be excited or anxious.

He turns to Anders. "Would you mind if I had a moment alone with Ella?"

Anders nods. "Okay."

He stands, grabs his cane, then navigates out of the break room and into the Jump Hangar.

Grandfather sits in the chair next to mine, takes my hands, and meets my eyes.

Is something wrong?

Did something happen to my father?

"I need you to do something, but I'm not sure if you're ready."

"What is it?"

"I wouldn't ask this if there were anyone else with a splinter of your talents."

I sit up, smiling a bit as I nod, lapping up the acknowledgment.

"There's no other way than just to come out and say this …" He draws a deep breath. "We need you to eliminate a target."

I *must* have heard him wrong.

I wait for the punchline, but there's no smile on his face, and the light has left his eyes.

"You need me to *kill* someone?"

"His name is Joe Norwood. He's a dangerous Deviant who is about to do some terrible things."

I look at Grandfather, then at Eden, who is staring back at me blankly. It's weird. Her face is usually so expressive that you can forget that she's not a real person. But then there are moments like now where she stares with a vacancy to betray the illusion.

"You want me to *kill* someone? I thought we were about helping people. Spying on the bad guys, protecting people in danger? You never said that you kill people."

"We usually don't. But this is an extreme situation. We have it on good authority that Mr. Norwood is going to do something very, very bad if we don't intervene."

"So why not call the police or send someone else?"

"You know we can't call the police for something that hasn't happened yet. Most people don't even know we exist, so we must tend to things discreetly."

"You've done this before?"

"If I told you that killing a bad guy could save your father, would you do it?"

I nod.

"What if killing the same bad guy could prevent the deaths of thousands?"

"Thousands?"

"Yes, Ella. Thousands."

"I don't know. Maybe. It would depend on the situation."

"The situation is this, Ella. Mr. Norwood is a dangerous Deviant. One of the biggest threats to have ever existed. And we have a narrow window to get him. He's unconscious in a hospital bed. A run-in with the cops has left him in critical condition. We have to kill him before he wakes up. Once he does, he'll walk right out of that hospital and kill everyone in his way.

"Why do you want him dead?"

"Have you heard about the The First Front?"

I shake my head.

"They're a group of misguided anarchists who want to turn the world against us. They're militantly anti-Deviant, even though they're led by Deviants."

Eden hands me her tablet. The screen shows news links with headlines. I see a few before I turn away.

Child Found Decapitated in Oak Park

Family Killed In Suspected Arson

Infant Ripped From Womb and Shot by Homeless Man Who Then Turned Gun on Self

Gunman Opens Up Fire in Lake City Preschool Then Kills Self

"Those are all Deviant murders. Each of them committed by a Jumper for The First Front, each at the behest of Joe Norwood."

"Wait, they're *Jumpers?*"

"Yes, and they're led by this man. Norwood used to work with us a long time ago. Until he lost his mind and we fired him. A couple of years ago some of our Jumpers in the field started running into his Jumpers, trying to thwart our missions."

"How can he even *know* about our missions?"

"Norwood's a powerful psychic. I imagine they tap into the same Great Whatever that we're all tapping into. But instead of helping, he's trying to hurt as many people as he can. He's teamed up with a few other Deviants. While they claim to be political, most of their crimes are opportunistic, attempts to get money to fund and grow their operation. They've been actively recruiting any of our students that just couldn't cut it. They play into the victimization, offering those students a chance to get even with 'The Man.'"

"So, you want me to kill him? Why me?"

"Because he knows our other Jumpers. Even unconscious, he may be able to defend himself. But he's never met you. And you and Anders are one of our most powerful pairs."

"What did my father say?"

Grandfather sighs. "He's out of town recruiting a new student. But we both know your father. He's scared. He doesn't trust you to do anything. And I can't say I blame him. Watching your mother die scared him. Hell, it scared me. So, I'm almost positive that he'd say no. Maybe I could talk him into it if he were here, but we don't have that luxury. I need you to make an adult decision, Ella."

"I don't think I can kill someone. I mean, how would I even do it?"

"That's the easy part. You'd be in the body of one of the attending nurses. Inject an air bubble into his line then walk away. You'll be in and out in less than a minute. Nobody would ever know how it happened. Your host would never be caught or charged with anything. Our psychics have already given it a ninety-nine point seven percent success rate … if *you* do it. Anyone else and it falls to thirty-seven percent."

"Oh my God …"

"He knows our other Jumpers. You'd be nearly invisible."

I look back down at the tablet, scrolling through even more headlines from this man's many murders. "He ordered *all* of these deaths?"

"Yes. And he'll order more. The First Front won't be satisfied until they kill all of our kind, or at least all of our kind that don't fall right in line behind them. But you can stop it, Ella."

"I can't kill anyone. I'm sorry."

"It's okay, Ella." Grandfather sighs as he stands. "We'll try and find someone else. Maybe I can team Anders and one of the other Jumpers."

He hugs me, then heads toward the door. As an almost aside, he says, "And hopefully, Anders won't get hurt."

"What do you mean? I didn't think Anders *could* get hurt."

"Anders would usually be fine in a Jump. But if he's with another Jumper who wakes Joe, all bets are off. There's no telling what Norwood could do to him. But don't worry. I'm sure we'll figure something out."

He's halfway out the door.

I know he's manipulating me, and I hate him a little for it. But, at the same time, I don't want to disappoint him. Nor do I want anything to happen to Anders or any of the other Jumpers.

"Fine. I'll do it."

Grandfather turns and smiles. "Thank you, Ella. I knew I could count on you."

I STEP into the cylinder and relax into the cushioned interior. Anders is already in his cylinder, the glass door sliding down over him.

"Hey, Ella," he speaks into my head.

Hey, Anders. You ready for today's Jump?

"Yeah. Looks like a challenging one."

We've got this.

I wonder if his brief went into as much detail as mine did, or if he realizes the threat that Joe Norwood poses.

Eden comes over to me, attaching electrodes to my chest and sliding a halo over my head — all of these things designed to monitor my vitals and brain waves, to ensure they don't have a repeat of what happened to Eden so many years ago.

If something goes wrong, like a runaway heart rate or a

psychic attack from the host — which is theoretical and hasn't happened so far as I know — they're supposed to be able to wake me up, return my soul to my body.

I hope that I'll never *need* these precautions.

"Are you ready?" Eden asks.

"Yes," I say.

She steps back, and the glass slides down, sealing me into the cylinder.

Every time the door closes, claustrophobia takes over and sends my heart racing. Fortunately, the sleeping gas kicks in quick, and then I'm out, relying on Eden and Anders to control where I'll Jump.

Eden smiles at me through the glass.

My eyelids grow heavy.

Chapter Twenty-Two

ELLA SHEPHERD AGE 17

I'M in the body of a nurse named Stephanie Jenkins.

She's worried about three things: getting through the day without a drink, getting through her shift without much sleep, and providing for her daughter, so she doesn't have to work two jobs and go to school just to get by.

She's eating lunch in her car resting her eyes when I take over.

Some people are easier to take over than others. The tired ones are usually easiest.

I sit up in the seat, accessing her memories and searching for info on Joe Norwood.

I find it almost immediately.

He's resting after surgeons had to open his skull to ease the swelling in his brain after the cops roughed him up, or, as the records state after he "tripped and fell down the stairs" following his apprehension.

I get out of Stephanie's car and head inside, steeling myself for what I have to do.

I feel nauseous as I clock in, duck into a supply closet, then head down the hall, past the officer stationed outside, and into Joe's room.

In the photos, taken many years ago, Joe Norwood was a muscular, clean-shaven black man in his early forties. Now, lying unconscious in the hospital bed, he looks considerably older. His face is puffy and bruised, what I can see between the bandages and his scruffy salt and pepper beard.

Wires and monitors track his vitals. An IV bag is connected to a tube in his arm. At least he's breathing on his own.

As I stand here, it's hard to see a killer, a man who is behind the deaths of so many Deviants. All I see is a frail, aging man, edging death.

Anders speaks in my head. "Don't think about how he looks now. Everybody looks harmless in a hospital bed. You have to do it before someone comes."

My host's hands shaking, I grab the syringe I'd shoved down the front of Stephanie's pants, pop off the cap, then pull the stopper back to draw air into the shaft.

Injecting it into his tube will cause an embolism. Then I can duck out, sparing Stephanie from being caught.

I freeze, staring down at him, unsure if I can go through with this.

I've gone on several missions where I've had to fight bad people to keep them from harming someone that psychics at the Karma Project said needed protecting. I've broken bones, ruptured lungs, blinded, and burned bad people, never once feeling bad. I was protecting the innocent, after all.

But to take a life, particularly when it's passed out in a hospital bed?

Much more difficult.

"Come on," Anders says. "Before he—"

"Wakes," says another voice in my head.

A deep voice I've never heard.

"You've come to kill me? Did Arnold send you?"

Oh shit.

I call out to Anders, *Pull me out. Now!*

But I can't sense Anders. I think we've been disconnected.

Anders?

"He's gone," Joe says, laughing.

Shit. Shit. Shit.

I've never been on a Jump without a co-pilot.

I'm exposed, alone, afraid.

I don't usually feel fear because I know that no matter what happens to my host, I'll be okay. I'll wake up in my own body.

But I don't think that's true with a psychic in my head.

I have no clue what he can do to me.

Why the hell didn't I ask Grandfather just how dangerous this might be?

I stare at his body, looking for any sign of consciousness, but he still looks the same.

"Who sent ya?"

I don't respond.

"Talk!"

I drop the needle as a sharp pain rips through my head and sends me to my knees.

I cry out, hoping that the officer outside didn't hear.

It's not like he can help me. And if he does come in, he's going to see the needle and wonder what the hell I'm doing.

I try to focus through the pain, my eyes a blur of brightness, searching for the syringe.

My fingers seize on it.

I raise it up, intending to deliver its payload.

Then a sharper pain hurls me to my back.

My head smacks the floor with a *THUD!*

Pain floods me, makes me want to cry.

I swallow my vomit.

"I asked who sent ya? You're with Fairchild, ain't ya?"

Yes. Please, stop hurting me.

He laughs, "I ease up, you best not try that shit again. You do, and I will kill your ass. Understand?"

Yes.

After a long moment, the pain goes from blinding to restraining.

"Your voice … you're just a kid, ain't you?"

Yes. I'm only twelve.

I pray he can't sense a lie.

"What's your name?" His voice is loud, like he's standing right behind me, shouting.

Ella.

"Ella What? You one of those kids from the school?"

Ella Shepherd. And yes.

"Shepherd? Like Ben?"

Shit! He knows my father? I hope he doesn't hate him.

Yes. He's my father.

"Did Ben send you after me?"

He suddenly appears in my host's mind, circles me, looking me up and down. I'm not sure if he can see a representation of me, in which case he probably knows I'm older than I said. Or if he sees something else, maybe an aura like I see when Anders is sharing a mind.

In this space, Joe looks strong and intimidating, like he

159

did in his more youthful photos. Like the kind of guy who wouldn't think twice about snapping me in half.

No, it was Arnold Fairchild. My father works with the school. He has nothing to do with this program.

"Damn, I thought Arnold Fairchild had sunk pretty low, but recruiting kids like you for murder? I gotta be honest, Ella. I'm surprised your father green-lit this shit."

He doesn't know anything about it. I'm working with my grandfather behind his back.

Shit. I didn't mean to admit that.

More laughter. "Arnold Fairchild is your *grandfather?*"

Yes. Please don't hold it against me.

I'm crying inside, wondering how long before the cop comes to stop me, arrests Stephanie before *she* can finish the job.

More laughter. "This is just so rich."

What?

I feel like I'm part of some joke between people I don't understand. The way he's laughing, this guy *must* be crazy.

"Well, it's just interesting that you're working for the grandpa that ordered the death of your other grandpa."

What are you talking about?

"Did Ben ever tell you about his Pops?"

Yes. He said that he went crazy and got himself killed.

"Only part of the story. Yeah, he did that, but it wasn't him in control."

Who was it?

"Yours truly. Fairchild got scared when Ben's daddy took off with him. Because Fairchild needed your father to save your mother. He ordered me to kill him, make it look like he went nuts."

And you just did it? You killed his dad?

He laughs, "And you're here *why* again?"

I say nothing.

I'm still trying to decide if he's telling the truth.

I've always known my grandfather to be a stern, but kind man. Not even close to something so cruel.

But still, he asked me to kill a man in his hospital bed.

Would a good person do that?

"How many others have you killed?"

None.

"Don't lie to me."

I swear. He only sent me because you know the other Jumpers, you'd sense them.

"And he thought I wouldn't sense you?"

Right.

"He was wrong." He laughs. "Again. Tell me, did he give you a reason why I deserved to die?"

I'm not sure what to say, so I settle for the truth.

He said you're behind The First Front. That you ordered a bunch of people killed, including women and children.

Another laugh. "He says *I* ordered people killed? Fuck, the balls on Arnie."

So, you don't kill people?

"We do what Project Karma used to do, protecting innocents. Not trying to shape fate by choosing who lives and dies. We protect people from *all* of you."

They said that we're protecting the good guys from you.

"Honey, your grandfather and Advanced Dynamic are the *Bad Guys*. They're working to manage the Deviant population by enslaving those they can work with then killing anyone they see as a threat. Men, women, and children. So, Ella, did they tell you about the bodies under the school?"

Bodies?

"No, of course not. How about how many babies died in Project Yolo?"

What are you talking about?

"Child, there's plenty you don't even know. And I'm guessing your dad's still blindly obedient to the old man, too. Doesn't even see the shit they're doing."

My father is a good man. And I'm a good person.

"Except when you're killing defenseless men in their beds."

I swear, I didn't know any of this!

He stops, glares at me, then sighs. "Hell, I don't know what to do with you. I should kill your ass just to send a message, but I'm guessin' Arnie doesn't care too much about you, not if he sent you after me."

Please, don't kill me. I swear, I didn't know any of this.

"Do you believe me?"

I consider saying yes, but I know that if it seems like I believe him too easily, he might think I'm lying.

Then he'll kill me right here in this body.

And then what?

Will my soul die? Or will I be stuck in The Void like Eden?

"Well, do you believe me, Ella?"

I don't know what to believe. Nothing makes sense.

He nods, "Child, I'm not gonna kill you, out of respect for your father. But you need to tell him what's going on. Tell your father that he needs to ditch Arnie. And maybe if he does, you can both work with me."

Thank you.

"Don't thank me yet. You've still gotta keep Arnie from finding out what you know. Otherwise, he might kill you to keep this shit secret."

I want to argue that my grandfather would never hurt me.

But do I know him, or the people I've been working with? Has my entire life been a lie?

"And if you do decide to stay with the bad guys, tell

Arnie that he should send a fucking man to do the job next time — not a kid."

A sharp blast of pain, even worse than the first, rips through my skull.

I cry out.

I'm awake, back in the Jump Chambers.

My cylinder slides up from the ground, but the glass doesn't hiss open to release me like it usually does following a Jump.

I look around the empty room.

Anders' cylinder is also closed.

Is there a malfunction?

"Eden?"

Usually, she's here, waiting to greet us after a Jump.

But the Chambers are empty. And the room is only dimly lit with a soft red glow from the lights above.

"Eden?" I call out louder. "Anders?"

No response.

I send a psychic ping to see if he'll pick up. I can feel him nearby, in the way you might sense someone in a darkened room.

Anders?

"*What's going on?*" he asks in my head. "*Where's Eden?*"

I don't know. Did you hear what Joe was saying about Mr. Fairchild?

"*Yes. It can't be true, can it?*"

I'm not sure what to say. I don't know what to think. I need to talk to my father. But we have to keep this between us. Okay? Nobody can know. Got that?

A long silence.

Okay, Anders?

"*Okay,*" he says, though I'm not sure he's committed. I have to remember that to Anders my grandfather is an intimidating man. Someone you don't want to lie to or

163

disobey. Not someone to conspire against. Maybe I *should* be more intimidated than I am. And yes, I'm scared. But I also know that my father will know what to do. He'll take care of this.

Don't worry, Anders. Nothing is going to happen to you. My father will figure out what to do. Okay?

"Okay."

I look around the Chamber, getting frustrated. Where is Eden?

I call out again, hoping someone is listening to the radios installed in our cylinders.

Suddenly, movement.

Someone walking in the darkness, but I can't see who.

"Hello?" I call out, banging on the inside of the cylinder, not sure how much sound travels outside. It's heavily insulated with cushion and electronics beyond that. I'm guessing sound doesn't travel too far.

"Hello?"

The person in the darkness steps toward Ander's cylinder, red light revealing the stranger as none other than my grandfather.

"I'm so sorry," I hear him saying through the speakers.

"Sorry for what?"

A cold chill runs through me, my heart racing.

"So sorry that Joe told you."

Oh, God.

He knows.

"He's crazy, why would he even lie like that?" I say, acting like I'd never believe a word from the man's lying mouth.

"Nice try, Ella. But I heard your conversation with Anders. And I'm sorry, I can't allow you to tell your father."

Anders screams, in both the radio and my head.

"What are you doing?" I cry out, unable to see anything other than Grandfather staring at Anders through the glass.

He must be launching a psychic attack.

I've never seen my grandfather harm a fly, let alone another person, but Dad told me that Grandfather is a powerful Deviant, able to pry inside a person's mind and inflict telepathic pain.

"Stop!"

Anders cries out incoherently.

But Grandfather isn't stopping!

I bang on the inside of the cylinder. I call out for Eden.

"Help!"

Nothing.

And I listen as Anders' cries turn to chokes.

And then silence.

Anders?

Nothing.

Anders?

I can't feel him.

"Did you kill him?"

Grandfather doesn't respond.

Instead, he's approaching my cylinder.

My heart is pounding.

My mind is scrambling for escape.

There is no release lever inside the cylinder.

And Eden is nowhere in sight.

And it's not like I can fall asleep on command, especially not with Grandfather walking toward me, likely intending to silence me forever.

"Please!" I cry out, "I swear, I won't say anything."

"I'm sorry, Ella," he says. "I'm truly sorry."

And then I feel the pain.

Chapter Twenty-Three

Ben Shepherd Age 38

I'M in the car waiting for Walter to exit the gas station bathroom.

Walter is my partner on recruitment trips. His gift belies his appearance. To look at Walter, you'd see a tall, zit-faced overweight redhead in his late teens. The last kid in the world you'd expect to exude confidence. But Walter has a gift of persuasion. Talk to him long enough, and he'll convince you of anything. I bring him to close the deals I can't close, with parents who are resistant or afraid of sending their children to a school they never heard of with people who want to "help" them, which they believe is code for "experiment on."

I try to explain that our program is different. We never harm anyone. We truly want to provide a safe place for kids to explore their abilities in a controlled environment.

But not all parents are receptive.

We're usually left with two choices. We either leave the kid be, which we'll do for Deviants with minor abilities or, in the case of a Deviant with powerful potential, we bring Walter out to seal the deal.

Ever since the public became aware of Deviants last year, when a European scientist working for an agency similar to AD wrote a tell-all book about Deviants being among us, and the government using them as psychic spies, it's made our job both more difficult and easier.

More difficult because no parent wants their kid to be used as a political pawn.

Easier because the public has not responded well to learning about the Deviants among them.

Politicians are stirring up fear of The Other. Parents don't want their kids going to schools with freaks. And some kids have been bullied to death. The environment has never been more volatile or the situation so dire.

And that's where Walter comes in, telling parents what they want to hear — convincing them that we'll protect their kids. We're not like those evil European agencies and whatever it is they're up to. We're different.

It's a necessary lie.

We *are* different.

At least I try to tell myself.

But then I think of Niko and Irina.

After I ratted Irina out, she was brought to Aspen Falls. It was under the auspices of reuniting the girl with her brother, but also because she'd lied about her powers. She's more powerful than she'd let on, and that makes her a threat.

I haven't seen her in two years, ever since she stole my powers.

The few times I tried to get something out of Fairchild, to at least see if Irina is okay and not being treated like some lab animal, the old man told me it's not my concern. He reminded me that I made my choice when I left AD following Willow's death. "You made it clear to us that you don't want to work on Projects, so don't ask."

Which is just his way of trying to pressure me into working on Projects again.

He'd love nothing more than for me to work with Eden again on Project Karma. But I refuse. He's lucky that I let Ella work with them in a limited capacity, and that's only because she insists, and I want her able to control her abilities.

But I don't want her working on AD's political agendas.

And I don't want her spying or doing whatever top secret other things they're doing.

It's bad enough that I'm a recruiter.

Sometimes I wonder if I'm implicit in the things that happen to the Deviants who wind up in Aspen Falls.

I'm certainly responsible for Irina.

But then I tell myself it's better to be here, with some ability to control my daughter's destiny.

Because if I wasn't working for AD, then what would keep them from coming for Ella and forcing her to join their program?

I shake my head, reminding myself that despite Aspen Falls, we're doing good work.

We're the Good Guys.

We're working to protect Deviants from abuse. There are rumors out there of others mistreating Deviants. Organized crime, other governments. Forcing Deviants into lives of crime. Forcing them to be soldiers for their cause. Experimenting on them, just as the Nazis had done.

We're the Good Guys.

We're trying to help.

So I tell myself with every new kid.

For every case like Niko and Irina, there are two dozen good ones — kids who find purpose. Kids who no longer have to feel like rejects. Kids who get to feel special and appreciated for their talents. We shelter them from the worst of humanity. Most of them will go on to live normal lives. Some will get to fight the good fight — to help others like themselves. To protect our country from threats foreign and internal.

God, I've been drinking the Kool-Aid!

Walter is pushing his way out of the convenience store, a giant soda in one hand and a bag of salt and vinegar chips in the other.

He pulls the passenger side open and starts to get in.

Once he's settled into the seat, I stare at him.

"What?" he asks, oblivious.

"What did I say about salt and vinegar chips?"

He laughs, "That they smell like douche?"

"Exactly. Please go back and get something else."

"But these are my favorite," he says, and I can sense him wondering if he should charm me.

I raise my finger. "Don't you dare."

He gives me an innocent smile. "Dare what?"

"Don't try that shit on me. Go get something else."

I close my eyes so he can't make eye contact with me. "Go."

"Fine."

He sets his giant drink in the center console, then opens the door and gets back out with a long sigh.

"Try getting something healthy," I call out, feeling like a nagging parent. I can't help it. You spend enough time with a kid feeding himself into an early grave and you start to feel like *someone* should say something. His parents were never able to say no, something which I'm sure had something to do with his gift, so he has no discipline. It makes him a bit of a man-child who wouldn't last a day in the world minus his gift.

So I'm a hard ass whenever we take road trips together, encouraging him to put discipline into his life — at least as much as I can with a nineteen-year-old who doesn't have to do a thing I say.

But I think part of him likes me saying no. Otherwise, he would have long ago attempted to charm me.

And so far as I know, he hasn't even tried.

He comes back out with another bag of chips.

He opens the door, and before I can chide him, Walter looks into my eyes and says, "Relax, these are salt and vinegar. You like these, okay?"

I nod. "Yeah. Those are fine."

I start driving as Walter chomps away at his chips.

Weird, I never liked the smell of salt and vinegar, but now my mouth is watering. "Can I try one?"

He hands me a couple. I shove them into my mouth.

They're tart and sting my eyes, but they're surprisingly good.

"You like them," he says more than asks.

"Yeah. I like them."

We're almost to Lara's town when a call comes over the speakers. I look at the dashboard screen and see *ARNOLD FAIRCHILD*.

"Answer," I say.

"Hello, Ben?"

Something is wrong in his voice.

"Yeah, what is it Mr. Fairchild?"

"It's Ella. Something's wrong."

Chapter Twenty-Four

Ben Shepherd Age 38

THE ELEVATOR DOORS open to Sub-Level Three of AD on a sea of averted eyes.

"Where is he?" I ask.

They point toward the Project Karma wing.

My heart is pounding as I run down the hall toward the large double red doors that open into the Project Karma Hangar.

I hate that I can't run faster, that I've let myself get out of shape.

My mind is racing with horrible things that might have happened.

Where is Ella? Is she okay? What the hell was she even doing on a Jump today? She's not supposed to Jump when I'm out of the building.

I push my way past the guards who don't even attempt

to check my credentials like they have the other times I've come down here.

I open the doors.

And I see Arnold standing there beside two open, exposed, and empty Jump Chambers. Eden is standing behind him, staring at the ground, also unable to meet my eyes.

"Where is she?" I yell before I'm anywhere near them.

Arnold looks up at me. "She's gone."

"What do you mean *she's gone?*"

"On her last Jump, something happened. Same as Eden. Her body died in the Chamber."

"Where is she?" I scream, grabbing Arnold by his collar, wanting to choke the life out of him.

He falls backward, trying to slap my hands away, but I'm too full of rage to let go.

"Please," Eden says, "stop it. I'll take you to her."

She offers me her hand.

I reluctantly let go of Arnold.

He glares at me.

"Come," she says.

I refuse her hand, instead choosing to follow her.

She leads us — Arnold is following at a distance — from the Hangar to the medic's lab.

Ella and Anders are lying on a pair of beds, both dead.

I cry out as I race to her, feeling for a pulse, trying to sense something, anything I can grab, or coax life into.

But she has no pulse.

Her body is cold.

She's gone dark, no sign of a soul — just like Willow.

"What did you do?" I scream, launching myself at Arnold.

My body locks up before I can throttle him.

He meets my eyes and shakes his head.

He's using his powers to keep me from killing him.

"This won't solve anything, Ben."

"What did you have her doing?"

"Just a routine Jump."

"That killed them *both*?"

"I'm so sorry, son," he says, coming to hug my paralyzed frame. "I'm so, so sorry."

I want to hurt him for allowing Ella to be harmed.

I want to hurt that fucking robot in a child's dead body, the robot that acts like my friend, acts like my wife, has my wife's memories, but isn't my fucking wife.

I want to burn this whole fucking place to the ground.

But all I can do is sob while Arnold Fairchild hugs me.

Chapter Twenty-Five

Ben Shepherd

It's been two weeks since my daughter died.

I'm at my desk at the Academy. I told people I'd be in my office until five, so just another ten minutes until I can leave this place for good.

This awful place, part of AD even if the school has its own name, with its fucking secret government programs that live on even though three people devoted to it — four including Anders — are dead. People I loved, gone.

I don't even know why I stayed two weeks after the funeral, other than some sense of obligation to the children I work with and ensuring that my successor, a woman named Amanda Barrett, knows what the kids need.

I certainly didn't stay out of loyalty to Arnold Fucking Fairchild.

We haven't spoken since the day Ella died.

I didn't even talk to him at her funeral, despite his

attempt to console me, or "manage the situation," as it were.

The sooner I put this place behind me, the sooner I can start over.

I should never have come back.

I should've tried to find another way to help Ella with the Jumping. I'm sure I could've found *someone* to help that wouldn't get her involved in Project Karma. Maybe Kotke would've helped me in secret.

Instead, I let fear push me back into Arnold's arms.

At the funeral, Arnold spoke about how much Ella had loved her job. How she'd told Eden that the only time she ever truly felt alive was while working to help advance science.

Those words felt like a knife through my fucking heart.

It was my fault that she found joy in Jumping. Probably because she didn't find any at home. I was obsessed with my work, helping other kids, and making a difference in the world — never realizing that I wasn't making the proper difference at home with my daughter.

I've spent most waking moments at home going through Ella's things, getting drunk, and regretting the past decade or so.

After Willow's death, work became my life to the exclusion of everything else. No friends. No family. Only colleagues and students, none of whom I ever truly connected with.

Hell, the closest thing to a friend I have left is Eden, a fucking robot. My wife's memories inside her dead twin, frozen as a child for as long as she lives.

Even though it's not the real thing, it's good to be able to relive old memories with a clone of her brain. Hell, there are times I almost call her Willow.

I suppose it's a good thing that Willow's mind is in a

child's body and not a twin of my adult wife. The line might be too blurred. I might have allowed myself to believe that Willow wasn't gone. Might have fallen in love with a robot.

Eden has come by to check on me, a few times now during her weekly visits to the school where she works with a few of the shyer, more troubled kids. We have lunch in my office.

Sometimes we talk about work or the children. Other times I talk to "Willow," where she'll use a perfect replication of her voice, and it almost feels like the real thing.

Sometimes when we're done talking, I'm reminded that she's gone, and her death feels like a fresh cut.

On those days, I start drinking early.

The final few minutes of my last day mercifully pass without any unexpected calls or emergencies.

I sign off on the computer, push my chair back and stand, then give my office a goodbye with my eyes before grabbing the box with my personal shit from the floor.

I take the back way out to avoid running into any students wanting to say goodbye. We already had a "Farewell Lunch" earlier. Several students cried as they hugged me. A few staffers seemed like they'd miss me, too, though I doubt that's as much to do with liking me as preferring the status quo.

I make it outside to the parking lot, find my car, and pop the trunk.

I stop, startled to see that it isn't empty.

Eden is inside, lying down, finger to her mouth. "Shh, don't tell anyone."

"What are you doing in here?" I whisper, looking nervously around.

A few people are walking to their cars, so I can't yank

her out or carry on a conversation without drawing attention.

Hey, why does Mr. Shepherd have a child in his trunk?

"You've got to get out," I whisper.

"No. There's something you need to know. *Please*. Take me with you."

"I can't take you with me. You … you're AD property. They'll find you, and they'll arrest me for theft, kidnapping, or something."

"Please, it's about Ella."

I look around one last time to see if anyone's looking my way. A security guard drives by in his cart but doesn't even glance my way.

I look back down at Eden. "Okay. I'll take you to a park to talk, but after that, you're coming right back here."

I slam the trunk closed.

I hop in the car, shaking, as I pull out of my space and pull up to the manned gate on my way out. There are two armed security officers, and I can't help but think that they're going to stop me.

Stop me on my last day just to make sure I'm not running off with a billion dollar psychic AI stuffed inside a child's body.

Since I already turned in my security card, I can't just pull up to the farthest gate and drive off. I have to approach the guards and be let out.

I pull into the exit lane behind a red Toyota. It doesn't have school stickers on the car or tag, so I'm guessing it belongs to visitors. One of the guards leans toward the driver-side window to say something, then sends the Toyota on its way.

My turn.

I pull up, my heart racing.

I imagine Eden sneezing in the trunk.

The officer, a young man named Antonio, greets me with a smile. "Hey, last day, eh Mr. Shepherd?"

"Yes, I'm afraid so, Antonio. Time to retire so I can finally sleep in for a change."

"Come back and tell me what it's like, okay?"

"Will do," I say as he steps inside the booth to raise the gate.

"Good luck, Mr. Shepherd."

"Thanks, Antonio," I say, eager to get the hell out of here.

I pull forward, not too fast.

I'm almost out.

"Hey!" shouts a man from behind me.

Shit! They got me.

It's over.

I stop the car, bracing for the worst.

I look in the driver's side mirror to see the other guard coming out, a tall blond brick house of a guy named Ludvig.

I watch as he approaches, my heart about to burst.

Please don't ask me to open my trunk.

Please don't ask me to open my trunk.

Please don't—

"Mr. Shepherd?"

Can you step out of your vehicle please, and open your trunk?

I look up meeting his belt buckle in my face. Pistol in a holster beside it.

He leans down, his eyes burrowing into me.

He smiles wide, revealing a perfect set of pearly whites if ever I saw one. "I just wanted to say goodbye, Mr. Shepherd. And thanks again for helping Julia."

Shit. I forgot all about how I helped his sister, one of the students, deal with one of the rare cases of bullying we've had at the school.

"You're welcome." I meet his smile with my own and offer him my sweaty palm. "Take care, Ludvig."

We shake.

He says goodbye.

I pull away from the school eager to reach the park and learn what Eden wants me to know.

I PULL INTO THE PARK, searching for a desolate spot.

I find a place behind the tennis courts, hidden well enough behind other vehicles and a thicket of trees.

I stop the car, pop the trunk, and get out.

Eden is climbing out, long red hair falling over her face, making her look like a mischievous child sneaking away from school grounds.

"What's going on?" I ask.

"Let's get in the car."

"Okay."

I get in.

She sits in the passenger seat.

I turn the car back on, and the air blasts us. "Okay, talk."

She looks up at me with eyes that remind me so much of Willow's, and Ella's. It's even harder to look at her thinking of my lost daughter.

"I don't want you to leave," she says.

"It's too late. I need to go. All that I've lost is killing me there."

Her eyes start to water.

Hell, I never thought that Eden might miss me. I considered that I'd miss her, but it wasn't *her* I'd be missing. It was the proxy conversations with Willow.

And ultimately, I felt it was better to make a clean

break. If I let myself continue my friendship with "Willow" through Eden, then I'd never leave the school. I'd grow old and die, bitter and alone.

As I see Eden cry, I feel like an ass for not considering how she might feel. Though she was in large part machine, there was some part of the child who had died — some part of Eden — left inside her. And a clone of Willow's brain. All of that made her *something*, if not a person. *Right?*

Something with feelings that I'd not even considered.

Shit.

"I can talk to Mr. Fairchild, get him to give you another position if you want. Somewhere you'll never see me again if that's what hurts."

"It's not you. It's the whole place. I need to move on. Ella's the only reason I came back to work with Mr. Fairchild. And now she's gone."

"What if she wasn't?" Eden asks.

"What do you mean?" I'm getting annoyed.

Eden's voice changes, becoming Ella's. "Did you know that I cloned Ella's brain?"

My heart skips a beat when I hear Ella's voice on Eden's lips.

"Let me live with you. I can be her." Her voice changes to Willow. "I can be Willow. I can be both of them. You never have to be alone."

"Why did you clone her brain?"

In Ella's voice, she says, "Because I didn't want you to be sad. And, because I didn't want you to leave us."

"Leave you?" I ask, surprised to hear a computer program talking like a possessive lover demanding my attention.

"I missed you the first time you left. We missed you. Me and Willow. I wish that we didn't. While AD built my knowledge base and programmed me, and some of Eden's memories were reconstructed, for the most part, my whole memories, the ones I think of when I think of myself in any way, come from Willow. I am, for all practical purposes, her."

"Stop," I say, my voice on the verge of cracking.

"Stop what?" she asks, using Willow's voice.

I snap.

I lunge out, grabbing her by the throat, choking her. "You are not my wife. You are not Ella. Stop it!"

She cries out, in Ella's voice, "Please, Daddy, stop. You're hurting me."

My anger, now doused with gasoline.

I squeeze her throat tighter, wanting to shut her up for good. "*You're not her!* You're not either of them. *You're not even fucking human.*"

And then there's something in her eyes.

A flash of pain that reminds me of the first, and only, time I ever truly broke Willow's heart, after a terrible fight when I said something awful.

That same look is in Eden's eyes now.

I let go of my grip.

She stares at me, wounded, tears flowing down her cheeks.

"I'm sorry," I say.

She opens the door and gets out of the car.

"Wait," I call out.

The door slams shut, leaving me alone with my shame.

I watch as she walks away, fast, eager to put distance between us.

I feel awful. I want to apologize, but a part of me knows that it's best to stay put. Let her leave. Let her hurt; she'll get over it. It's best. A bandage ripped from a wound.

What are the alternatives? To apologize, and then

what? Take her with me? No way in hell that Arnold would ever allow that.

And why would I even *want* her around?

So I can converse with *two ghosts* instead of just one?

I watch her in my rearview as she nears the road.

The school isn't far. She should be fine.

Just let her go.

I look away from her reflection.

Tell myself she's not real.

She's a copy of my wife's brain, a copy of my daughter's.

Not the real thing.

A computer program, data driven responses based on a set criteria.

She looks real.

Sounds real.

But she's not a real person.

And she's not a replacement for either Willow or Ella, no matter how good it might feel to pretend.

A clever trick of technology.

Best to let her go.

A horrifying squeal rips my attention back to the street.

A UPS truck is stopped.

Car horns honking.

And … Eden is nowhere in sight.

I hop out of the car.

I race to the street.

I see beyond the shrubs, see Eden's crumpled body lying face down in the street.

Oh, God.

Blood pouring from her.

I run faster.

The driver is out of his truck.

Cars are stopped.

I keep running.

I'm there first, falling beside her.

"Eden!" I cry out, turning her over.

Her face is bloody, smashed beyond recognition.

I swallow, grief splintering my body, leaving fragments in my soul.

"I'm so sorry," I cry, cradling her limp body, my face against her broken face. "I'm so sorry."

People are talking to me, but I can't hear what they say.

Instead, my attention is drawn to Eden's hand, her little fingers twitching.

I take her hand, squeezing it, flashing back on the many times I'd held Willow's hand just like this.

And Ella's.

Her fingers squeeze tighter.

What?

I look down and see an aura, a pink one, surrounding her.

Until now, Eden's aura has always had a similar mix of signatures, a blend of the girl that she was and her hardware's program.

It wasn't human. It had a distinct hum and a constant green aura, not like a soul's, but some nebulous combination of body and tech.

But this light inside her feels different. Looks different. A bright pink like Willow's soul, tinged with violet like Ella's, with specks of green and red swirling inside.

It is … somehow … *a soul*.

How is this possible?

Her fingers squeeze tighter. A blinding light and pain rip through me.

I try to close my eyes, but it's impossible to smother my mind.

A rush of memories storms my senses. A chaotic

churning of sights and sounds and tastes and smells. A rush of emotions threatening to drown me.

So many. Too fast. A torrent I'm forced to swallow, else I choke.

But I can't process a thing.

Ella's memories. Willow's. Eden's.

She's uploading them to me.

And then, all is silent.

I watch as the light rises from her chest, hovering in front of me.

I feel its warmth. Impossible radiance on my face.

Then it blinks from existence.

And I'm alone, but no longer alone. I'm with the collected memories of Willow, Ella, and Eden, all in my head, swarming, making me dizzy as I try to control them, to slow them to a quiet roar.

It's like a stream of data I must slow to understand it better.

People approaching. A siren in the distance. Someone, a man, asks if she's okay. But their voices are dull as if heard by someone else.

A part of me is seeing and hearing the voices and memories of my wife, her sister, and my daughter.

Eden's terrible visions storm my mind, and then I learn the horrible truth of what Fairchild has done to my father and daughter, and what he plans to do to humanity.

And I'm the only one who can stop him.

Epilogue

ELLA

~

I STARE at my father as he lets go of my head.

The surge of memories fades to a trickle.

I look up at him. "I'm … I'm not Ella?"

He shakes his head. "No."

"Then who am I?"

"I think you're the pink thing that I saw when Eden was dying. Energy? A soul? Or something new. I don't know."

I swallow, trying to comprehend all that I've seen, all that I've felt, all that he's uploaded into my head.

I feel a hundred different things, but not one of them is good.

All I can think is, *I'm not real.*

I'm not real.

I'm not—

An explosion tears through the main hall, followed by gunshots and screams.

"They've found us," Ben whispers, grabbing his gun.

A Quick Favor...

If you enjoyed this book, please take a moment to write a short review on your favorite online bookstore so other readers can enjoy it, too.

Thanks so much!

About the Authors

Sean Platt is an entrepreneur and founder of Sterling & Stone, where he makes stories with his partners, Johnny B. Truant, and David W. Wright, and a family of storytellers.

Sean is the bestselling author of over 10 million words' worth of books, including the Yesterday's Gone and Invasion series. Sean is also co-author of the indie publishing cornerstone, Write. Publish. Repeat. and co-host of the Story Studio Podcast.

Originally from Long Beach, California, Sean now lives in Austin, Texas with his wife and two children. He has more than his share of nose.

David W. Wright is the co-author of edge-of-your seat thrillers including the best-selling post-apocalyptic series *Yesterday's Gone*, the paranoid sci-fi *WhiteSpace* series, and the vigilante series, *No Justice*, as well as standalone thrillers *12*, and *Crash* which was recently optioned for a movie.

David is an accomplished, though intermittent, cartoonist who lives in [LOCATION REDACTED] with his wife and son [NAMES REDACTED.]

He is not at all paranoid.

He is "the grumpy one" on the *The Story Studio Podcast* with fellow Sterling and Stone founders, Sean Platt and Johnny B. Truant.

David writes about books, TV shows, movies, and

video games he enjoys; his struggles with anxiety and OCD; writing; and posts the occasional drawing at his personal blog at davidwwright.com

You can email him at david@sterlingandstone.net

We swear, he almost never bites. Unless you feed him after midnight.

For a full list of his most recent books visit sterlingandstone.net.

Also By Sean Platt

The Dead World Series

Dead Zero

Dead City

Dead Nation

Dead Planet

Empty Nest

The Beam Series

The Beam Season One

The Beam Season Two

The Beam Season Three

Robot Proletariat Series

En3my

Robot Proletariat

The Infinite Loop

The Hard Reset

Cascade Failure

Reboot

The Tomorrow Gene Series

Null Identity

The Tomorrow Gene

The Tomorrow Clone

The Eden Experiment

Karma Police Series

Jumper

Karma Police

The Collectors

Deviant

The Fall

Homecoming

Yesterday's Gone

October's Gone

Yesterday's Gone Season One

Yesterday's Gone Season Two

Yesterday's Gone Season Three

Yesterday's Gone Season Four

Yesterday's Gone Season Five

Yesterday's Gone Season Six

Tomorrow's Gone

Tomorrow's Gone Season One

Tomorrow's Gone Season Two

Tomorrow's Gone Season Three

Available Darkness

Darkness Itself

Available Darkness Book One

Available Darkness Book Two

Available Darkness Book Three

WhiteSpace

WhiteSpace Season One

WhiteSpace Season Two

WhiteSpace Season Three

Stand Alone Novels

Burnout

The Island

Crash

Emily's List

Pattern Black

Devil May Care

The Secret Within

Also By David W. Wright

Cold Vengeance

Cold Vengeance

Cold Reckoning

Hidden Justice

Hidden Justice

Hidden Honor

Hidden Shame

Hidden Virtue

No Justice

No Justice

No Escape

No Hope

No Return

No Stopping

No Fear

Karma Police

Jumper

Karma Police

The Collectors

Deviant

The Fall

Homecoming

Yesterday's Gone

October's Gone

Yesterday's Gone Season One

Yesterday's Gone Season Two

Yesterday's Gone Season Three

Yesterday's Gone Season Four

Yesterday's Gone Season Five

Yesterday's Gone Season Six

Tomorrow's Gone

Tomorrow's Gone Season One

Tomorrow's Gone Season Two

Tomorrow's Gone Season Three

Available Darkness

Darkness Itself

Available Darkness Book One

Available Darkness Book Two

Available Darkness Book Three

WhiteSpace

WhiteSpace Season One

WhiteSpace Season Two

WhiteSpace Season Three

Stand Alone Novels

Crash

Emily's List

Threshold

The Secret Within